Anton

The Rebellion Series

Nicola Jane

Copyright © 2020 – Original Edition by Nicola Jane.

Copyright © 2023 – Second Edition by Nicola Jane.

All rights reserved.

No portion of this book may be reproduced in any form without written permission from the publisher or author, except as permitted by U.K. copyright law.

Meet the Team

♥

Cover Designer: Francessca Wingfield@Wingfield Designs
Editor: Rebecca Vazquez, Dark Syde Books
Formatting: Nicola Miller

Disclaimer

This book is a work of fiction. The names, characters, places, and incidents are all products of the author's imagination and are not to be construed as real. Any similarities are entirely coincidental.

Spelling Note

NICOLA JANE

Please note, this author resides in the United Kingdom and is using British English. Therefore, some words may be viewed as incorrect or spelled incorrectly, however, they are not.

A note from the Author

♥

I don't feel this book needs a warning. If you read Mafia/MC romance, you already know what to expect. But for the people out there who require one, consider yourself warned. This book isn't for the faint-hearted.

Acknowledgments

Thank you to my readers who love whatever I write. I appreciate every comment, share, review and TikTok x

Contents

Playlist	IX
Prologue	1
Chapter One	3
Chapter Two	18
Chapter Three	33
Chapter Four	48
Chapter Five	65
Chapter Six	79
Chapter Seven	96
Chapter Eight	118
Chapter Nine	135
Chapter Ten	146
Chapter Eleven	164
Chapter Twelve	182

Chapter Thirteen	196
Chapter Fourteen	218
Chapter Fifteen	242
Chapter Sixteen	263
Chapter Seventeen	281
Chapter Eighteen	303
Chapter Nineteen	318
Chapter Twenty	334
Chapter Twenty-One	352
About the Author	361
Social Media	362
Also by Nicola Jane	363

Playlist

♥

Bad Thing – Jesy Nelson
Boyz – Jesy Nelson ft. Nicki Minaj
A Year Ago – James Arthur
Someone To You – Banners
Take Care – Drake ft. Rihanna
Torn – Natalie Imbruglia
Head Over Feet – Alanis morissette
Iris – The Goo Goo Dolls
21 Questions – 50 Cent ft Nate Dog
Mesmerize – Ja Rule ft. Ashanti
Love Don't Cost A Thing – Jennifer Lopez
I Guess I'm In Love – Clinton Kane
The Way You Do The things You Do – UB40

Prologue

PIPER

I step through the door to the clubhouse, my arms laden down with bags. I spot Hulk, the club's VP, and Ace, the President, sitting by the bar. Ace smiles and asks, "You been shopping?" I don't miss the way Hulk rolls his eyes in irritation when Anton follows me inside.

"This woman is a shopaholic," Anton mutters.

"You letting the Mafia buy your shit?" Hulk snaps, looking back over his shoulder at me.

"I can treat my woman to whatever she likes," says Anton with a smirk. "Maybe you should have done this, then she wouldn't have gotten tired of your arse."

Hulk growls. "I wasn't talking to you."

Ace leans into Hulk and mutters words that I don't quite catch, but I assume he's telling him to calm the fuck down.

I sigh, taking the opportunity to quietly tell Anton, "Let's go to my room." Then, I breeze past Hulk, ignoring him. I'm becoming an expert at handling his tantrums.

"You need to stop ignoring me, Piper," growls Hulk angrily. He waits a beat before adding, "Or I'll tell him everything." I stop in my tracks and spin to face him. Our eyes lock, and we're in a silent standoff.

"Piper," Anton says, "what the hell's he talking about?"

Chapter One

♥

Six months earlier...

Piper

I slam the shot glass down on the shiny bar top and signal for the bartender to fill it up again. I can tell by his face he's weighing up whether to serve me or turf me out. I arch a brow, daring him, and he reluctantly fills my glass with sambuca. "You should just leave the bottle here," I slur and pick up the glass. The sticky liquid spills over my fingers as I drink it in one go.

"I think you should call it a night," he suggests gently.

"I think that's way above your paygrade," I snap. "To stop me drinking, you'd need danger money." He reluctantly tops up my glass again and then moves away. I watch him speak into his radio, and I scowl at him. *Party pooper.*

A girl dressed in next to nothing brushes past me as she reaches behind the bar and takes a bottle of vodka. "I'm taking this for the girls," she says, waving it at the bartender. He nods, barely looking in her direction as he speaks quietly into his radio.

I throw a twenty on the bar top. "Don't worry, I'm leaving," I tell him. I stand and grip the bar to steady myself before following the girl with the vodka. We head backstage, but she doesn't notice me until I'm in the dressing room with her.

She smiles. "Are you the new girl?" I shrug and return her smile. This seems to be the right answer because she unscrews the cap and hands me the bottle. "You can go first. Welcome to the team."

A few minutes later, I'm introduced to some of the other dancers, and then I'm taken to another room bustling with half-naked women doing makeup and getting changed. "The new girl's here," shouts my vodka friend, and another woman rushes over, looking harassed. She grabs me by the shoulders and looks me up and down.

"There's not much on you," she mutters before reaching over to a nearby rail full of clothes. She retrieves a short, sparkly dress and holds it up in front of me. "Perfect." Then she thrusts it into my chest. "Hurry, you're on it three."

"Three?" I repeat, my eyes wide.

"She means three minutes," explains vodka girl. "Sandra, by they way," she adds, holding out her hand, which I shake.

"Did you not hear me, new girl? Hurry," snaps the other woman.

"That's Paris. She's the boss's pet but thinks she's actually the boss. It's best to do what she says, though, because she holds the power to fire you," whispers Sandra.

Another woman rushes over. "Christ, you're wasted," she comments, spinning me away from her and unfastening the zipper on the dress I'm currently wearing. "Paris needs you out there in one minute." She tugs my dress down, and I step out of it. She turns me back to her. "What the hell are you wearing?" she hisses, eyeing my underwear. I frown, looking down at the cotton knickers and unmatched white bra. "Fuck me, Sandra, grab us something off the rack."

Sandra grabs my boob. "C," she announces, looking proud when I nod. She takes a black lace bra and thong and removes the store labels. The other woman begins removing my bra, and I try to cover my boobs as she laughs.

"A shy one? That's a first."

Once I'm tucked into the new underwear, I step into the sparkly dress just as Paris rushes back over. "Now, new girl. Get on stage."

"Stage?" I repeat.

She growls and grabs me by the wrist, leading me through the room and up three steps. "Now, keep the knickers on. That way, they'll stick around to see what you're hiding. We'll put you back on later."

"Erm, I think there's been some kind of—"

"What's your stage name?" she asks, cutting me off.

"But I don't . . . I haven't—"

"Forget it, just get out there," she hisses, shoving me forward.

I stumble out and cheers erupt, making me jump in fright. A bright light is shone in my

ANTON

direction, and I automatically cover my eyes. "Gentlemen, we have a real treat for you this evening. She's new, she's shy, and she's fresh out of college. Give it up for Sweet V." The voice booms from the speakers, and I wince as men cheer in delight.

Music begins to play. "Fucking move," hisses a voice from the left side of the stage. "What the hell's wrong with you?"

I take a few steps to the centre of the stage, taking comfort in the fact the stage light is so bright, I can't see any of the crowd. "Dance," the voice growls impatiently.

I take a deep breath and close my eyes. I came here to forget, and this is certainly a good distraction. I picture Hulk, the guy I've been lusting over since I was a teenager, and a smile plays on my lips. I've only ever danced for him, and God knows how he'd react if he could see me now. I begin to sway to the soft beat of the music, occasionally dipping my hips. It would serve Hulk right if he saw me up here—he treats me like shit, yet he'd still hate this. His jealousy would force him to react.

As I move, I run my hands up my thighs, lifting the dress higher. A few men whistle, and it spurs me on. I lift the material higher until it's over my stomach, then I turn my back on the crowd. I have a good arse—it's one of the things Hulk fixates on—So I lift the dress over my head and drop it to the ground. I turn back to the crowd, cupping my breasts while swaying and dipping low. The music is about to end, so I slip the bra straps from my shoulders before unfastening the back and removing it completely.

The loud cheers deafen me, and once the music stops, I smile bashfully before heading off the stage. Paris spins me back around, telling me, "Collect your cash, new girl."

The stage lights are off, and I feel more exposed now that I can see the faces of the audience. A security guy in a black suit is standing in front of the stage, holding up a bunch of notes for me to take. "I collected them as you danced. You don't want any of the other girls taking them on your first day," he says with a wink.

"Thanks." I smile, then leave the stage quickly.

I change back into my own clothes, and then a vodka bottle is thrust into my hand. "How much did you make?" asks Sandra.

ANTON

"I haven't counted it," I say, stuffing the cash straight into my bag as the reality of what I've just done hits me hard. I gulp down some of the vodka and then pass it back to her.

"You never told me your name," she says.

"I'm Piper." The night's alcohol is threatening to make a reappearance, and I'm pretty sure I should make my exit now before I'm shoved back out there.

"Who the hell are you?" A redhead stalks towards me with her eyes narrowed.

"Piper," I tell her.

"Relax, Cassie, she's the new girl," says Sandra.

"Really? Because I have a woman out front telling me she's here for the trial and her name matches the one I've been given."

Sandra smirks but waits for me to speak. Before I can, a security man steps into the room. "The boss wants to see the new girl," he grunts.

The redhead throws her hands up in despair. "Wouldn't we all," she huffs.

"I should just go," I murmur, trying not to draw any more attention to myself.

"He means you," the redhead snaps. "The boss wants to see you. God only knows what he'll do to me, putting an amateur on the stage."

"Come with me," orders the security guy.

I glance at Sandra again, and she holds her hands in the air, still smirking. "You're on your own with that one, I'm afraid."

I follow him back through the bar and up some stairs. We pass the turn for the VIP area and, instead, we stop at a door opposite, the word 'Office' displayed on the front. The guy knocks once, and a deep voice tells us to enter. I wipe my sweaty palms on my dress. I feel the alcohol wearing off with each step and dread is filling me.

The door opens and the security guy stands to one side, allowing me to step in. I gasp at the sight of Anton Martinez sitting behind the desk. *Fuck.*

ANTON

I don't bother to look up as she enters. I continue to count some cash before wrapping a band around it and throwing it onto the pile. Eventually, I look up and nod to the security guy for him to leave, which he does. I pile up the stacks of cash and slide them into my desk drawer before letting my eyes fall to Piper. Her head is lowered, and her eyes are fixed to the floor. She clearly didn't realise I own this place because, right now, she looks like she wants the ground to swallow her up.

"Sit," I order, then I wait a few beats while she lowers into the chair opposite my desk. "How the fuck did you get out of a club that's supposedly on lockdown?" I spoke to Hulk, the Vice President of The Rebellion MC, just an hour ago and he never mentioned the club princess was AWOL.

"They're all busy looking for Ace and Mae," she mutters.

The club's President was taken along with a club member's daughter. So far, there have been no leads, and it's been a few days. "Meanwhile, you're here getting your tits out for money?"

"That was an accident," she almost whispers. "I didn't mean for that to happen."

I lean back in my chair and watch her fidget uncomfortably. "How the fuck do you dance on a stage in front of hundreds of men, get half-naked, and not mean to do it?"

I think I see the hint of a smile before she chews down on her lip. "Well, I was having a drink at the bar and I followed one of the dancers backstage. Somehow, she thought I was a new dancer, and then I was kind of bustled onto the stage." She pauses, looks up at me, and shrugs her shoulders. "Sorry."

I can't help but laugh. "So, my girls forced you on stage, is that what you're telling me?"

"It was a misunderstanding."

"Would it have anything to do with the fact you're wasted?"

"I just needed to let my hair down. Things have been intense at the club."

"I take it no one knows you're here?" She shakes her head. "I should call Hulk."

She straightens up. "No, please don't do that."

"Don't you think your boyfriend hates me enough without me keeping this from him?" I arch a brow. Hulk hates the Mafia, he's made that perfectly clear, but the agreement I have is with his father, Ace.

"He's not my boyfriend," she mutters.

"Does he know that?"

"Look, I promise not to come back here. I didn't know you owned it. I just thought it would be a good place to hide out for a few hours."

ANTON

I snigger. "On a normal Saturday, this place would be full of your biker friends. You're lucky they're preoccupied."

"Can we keep this between us?" she asks, peeking at me through her lashes.

I scoff. "You don't have anything I need." She frowns. "That's how it works, sweetheart. I keep your secrets, and you repay me somehow." I pause for a beat and grin. "And it's not the first secret I have of yours, is it? It's becoming a habit."

"Anton, please," she pleads.

I lean back in my chair. I have a plan forming that could work this to my advantage. "What would Bear and Queenie say about their daughter dancing in a strip bar?"

"They don't need to know," she snaps.

I turn my laptop to her, pressing play on the CCTV video of her dancing. She immediately looks away, blushing. "Who knew you were hiding all that under there?"

"What do you want?"

"I haven't decided."

"I could tell Tag about this," she threatens, and I laugh hard.

"You realise Tag is below me, right? In the chain of command, I'm the top. The *very* top."

"Please," she whispers, "you can't show anyone that video."

I bridge my fingers and rub them over my lips like I'm thinking. "I need a date for tomorrow night. You will be my date."

She looks surprised. "Date?" she repeats.

"Yes. Be ready for noon tomorrow. You'll need to be fitted for a dress, so I'll have someone pick you up. Don't let me down, Piper, or I will send this recording to every member of The Rebellion."

There's a knock on the door, and I order them to enter. Cassie struts in, flicking her long red hair behind her shoulder confidently. She glances at Piper with disdain. "I am so sorry, Mr. Martinez. I'm not sure what happened."

"I do," I snap. "You let a stranger walk in off the streets and dance in my club."

"She said she was the new girl," Cassie argues.

"Look, Anton, this was all my fault, I—" begins Piper, but I hold up my hand to stop her from speaking and the words die on her lips. She gives Cassie an apologetic look.

ANTON

"Oh, I know whose fault this is, Piper," I growl. "Michael will take you home. Cassie, show her out." The women waste no time in escaping.

As the door is closing, it swings back open and Tag saunters in. His eyes are glazed and he's holding a glass of amber liquid loosely in his hand. He drops down in the seat Piper just vacated. "Something bothering you?" I ask.

"My wife won't talk to me, I haven't seen my kid in days, and we're still missing the President of The Rebellion."

Tag's alliance to the club runs way deeper than mine since he married the President's daughter. He's under pressure to get answers for his wife.

"She's still blaming you for all this?" I guess.

"Apparently, it's my fault her dad and her friend are missing. I mean, we don't even know who's behind it, and she's blaming me." He sighs. "How can two people just disappear off the face of the earth?" He rubs his forehead and groans. "She keeps cancelling my time with Abel."

"She'll relax once they're home, and they *will* come home, Tag. We'll make sure of it. We've got men out there doing everything possible." I lean forward. "Guess who was in here just now."

He shrugs. "Piper."

Tag raises an eyebrow. "Interesting. Alone?"

I nod. "Yep. Dancing on stage."

Tag grins, and it's the first smile I've seen on his face in days. "No fucking way. Did she strip?"

"Top half," I say. "How'd yah think Bear would react to that?"

Tag laughs. "I think she'd be the first twenty-five-year-old to get grounded by her parents."

"Don't tell anyone, not even Lucy. I plan to use this to my full advantage."

"How?" Tag asks suspiciously.

"I'm taking her to the dinner tomorrow evening."

"To meet the families?" asks Tag, and I nod. He throws his head back and laughs hard. "Do I dare ask why?"

"You know they're getting restless. Maybe seeing me with a woman will settle them."

"For how long?"

I shrug. "I've never introduced them to a woman, so it should be enough to make them think this is serious, that I'm taking my role seriously." As the head of the families, I'm expected to marry and have children, mainly a son, so my name and bloodline will continue.

"And long-term?" he asks.

"I haven't gotten that far in my plan."

"Using Piper will cause an outright war with the club. Hulk already hates you."

"When an opportunity falls in your lap, you have to take it. The fact I can piss Hulk off at the same time is a double bonus. Besides, I got a glimpse of her hot body tonight and I'm not ready to forget it just yet."

Tag shakes his head. "I thought I was fucked-up."

Chapter Two

♥

PIPER

"Where the fuck did you go last night, Piper?" Hulk is pacing the room as anger pulsates from him. My mum glares at me, silently urging me to answer. "You're a fucking selfish bitch," he adds, his voice getting louder.

"I needed to get out of here," I explain. "It's intense right now, in case you haven't noticed."

He scoffs, stopping to glare down at me. "Oh, I fucking noticed, Piper. We all have. My dad is missing—the President of this club. Don't you think I want to slip out of here and get wasted? And what about Bernie? Don't you think she's missing Mae? We're all feeling it, Piper, but we're not all running out and drinking and partying, because the brothers are under enough

ANTON

pressure right now without searching the town for your selfish arse."

"Christ, what's the big deal? No one even noticed anyway."

"Shit, now you're pissed we were too busy to notice?" he asks in disbelief. "Ain't it time you acted your age? I mean, you're a little old for attention seeking."

"You've made your point, Hulk," I snap.

He leans closer until his face is inches from my own. "Do not leave this club without my say so. Are we clear?" I nod. "I said, are we clear?" he yells.

"Yes!" I shout back. "Loud and fucking clear. Message received."

Hulk storms from the room, and Mum lets out a breath and sighs. "What the hell were you thinking, Pip?"

"Clearly, I wasn't," I snap. "Stupid Piper, always running off and getting herself into trouble." Mum reaches for my hand, but I pull it away. "I'm so tired of all this."

"He's trying to protect us," she says carefully. "If anything were to happen to you, Hulk would never forgive himself."

"You're kidding yourself if you think he's doing this for me. Hulk hates me, and we all know it, so stop pretending he's suddenly my knight in shining armour."

"That's enough." My dad rises from the corner of the room. He reminds me of a Viking with his fiery hair and bushy ginger beard.

"Bear, leave it. She's just upset," Mum mutters.

"No, Queenie, I won't leave it. Piper, you're behaving like a spoiled brat. Sort your shit out or I'm sending you away to Aunt Callie in Scotland."

My eyes go wide at his threat. It's been a good few years since he last used that line on me. "Pops, I'm twenty-five. You can't send me away."

"I'll send you where the fuck I like if it keeps you safe. I can't have you upsetting the VP when he's already under enough pressure."

"Christ. What is this? Saint fucking Hulk Day? Did I miss the memo?"

"Hulk's doing a damn good job of keeping this club going while his dad, our President, is fuck knows where. The least you owe him is some damn respect." He storms out too, and I groan.

Mum presses her lips together. "Two men in less than five minutes. You'll be nicknamed

ANTON

Medusa if you continue slaying the guys like that." She smirks, and I roll my eyes.

"I just needed a break from it all, ya know?" A tear rolls down my cheek and I swipe it away angrily. "I just keep thinking about Mae and if she's scared or . . ." A sob escapes. "Or what if she's already . . ." I cry into my hands.

Mum gently rubs circles on my back. "We have to stay strong and remain positive. She's got Ace with her, and he'll do whatever it takes to protect her, you know that."

I take a calming breath. "I need to go out tonight. Hulk's going to lose his mind."

"Where?"

"I owe Anton a favour. He's calling it in."

Mum holds me at arm's length and frowns. "I thought there was nothing between you guys?" There's been a few times where Anton's acted like we were a thing, mainly to piss off Hulk since they hate one another. But then Anton helped me out one time, and Mum made me swear there was nothing between us.

"I owe him, Mum. You know he's helped me out, and when he calls it in, I have no choice. He's sending a car to collect me at noon."

"I think it'll be fine, but run it past Hulk, so he doesn't feel like Anton's ruling this place. His main concern is your safety, and he knows you'll be safe with Anton."

I nod, pushing to stand and heading for the office. I may as well get it out the way now. I knock to get his attention, and he glances up and groans loudly. "Sorry. I just need to run something by you."

"Make it quick."

"Anton is sending a car for me in," I glance at my watch, "ten minutes. He needs my help tonight."

Hulk's temple pulsates, a sure sign he's about to explode. "Help with what?"

"He asked me to be his date for the evening, but before that, he's sending someone to take me dress shopping."

Hulk smirks, and I brace myself for his nasty comment, but instead, he pulls out his mobile phone and dials a number. He relaxes into his chair. "So, now you're chasing Rebellion women?" he asks, and I roll my eyes. He's calling Anton. "Well, I need to know what security you're putting on her." He waits for another beat before disconnecting the call. "Have a great time," he tells me, going back to staring at his laptop.

"I can go?"

"Just stay safe, Piper," he mutters. "I don't need anyone else going missing."

I head out into the car park of the clubhouse. There's a sleek black car outside the gates, and as I approach, the back passenger door opens and Ella, Anton's sister, steps out. "Nice to see you again, Piper." Her blonde ponytail swings as she bounces towards me and wraps me in a hug. I'm slightly taken aback by her forwardness.

"Ella." I smile, patting her awkwardly on the back.

"I have Anton's credit card, so we're set for a fantastic shopping trip." She takes my hand and pulls me into the vehicle. "I love shopping."

"Is this shopping trip necessary? I have a nice dress that I could wear."

Ella smiles. "You're joking, right?" When I shake my head, she looks confused. "Anton gave me his credit card. That never happens. We need to take full advantage of it."

I stare out the tinted window at the passing shops. "I don't know how I feel about taking his money."

"Wow. I've never met anyone like you." Ella laughs and shakes her head. "Wait 'til I tell my girls."

An hour later, I step out of the dressing room in a figure-hugging black cocktail dress. Ella's mouth falls open. "That's it. That's the one." Relief floods me. This is the third shop we've been in and the sixth dress I've tried on. The others were either 'too loose' or 'not right', according to Ella, who seems to be a bit of a shopping expert. "Let's get it."

I rush back to the change room and get back into my clothes before she can change her mind. When I get out into the store, Ella is still browsing. "Right, I'm ready," I announce.

She holds up a pile of things. "Let's pay. I got you a few things to go with the dress."

ANTON

"I really don't need anything else." But Ella is already heading over to the cash desk and dumping the pile in front of the cashier. I carefully lay the dress on top. "What is all this stuff?" I ask, hooking my finger in a matching lace underwear set and dangling it in the air.

"You have to have good underwear to feel beautiful."

"Anton said I needed a dress. I don't need all this other stuff."

The cashier seems to hurry to scan the items before I make Ella put them all back. I notice a clutch with matching shoes. The dress alone is over four hundred, so it comes as no surprise when the cashier tells us the total is over a thousand pounds.

I curse, and Ella laughs. "He can afford it. Don't worry."

"I don't want him to think I've taken advantage."

Ella ignores me and takes the bags from the cashier. The bodyguard who's tailing us takes them from her as we leave the store. "We need to get back to the house, Lewis," she tells him. The driver opens the car door, and we climb inside. "The makeup artist is meeting us there shortly."

"Makeup artist?" I repeat, groaning.

"Yes. You can't meet the families looking less than perfect," she tells me.

"The who?" I ask.

"The caporegimes." When I'm still looking at Ella blankly, she laughs. "The made men. They all work under Anton, he's top dog, but they're all very important within the organisation, they head up smaller divisions."

"Why am I meeting them?"

"That's your date with Anton. You're his plus-one this evening."

I let that information sink in as we head to the house where Anton lives and I car drives down into an underground garage. I follow Ella and Lewis to the elevator, and we stand in silence as the cart rides up into the house.

The doors slide open into a large, busy kitchen where chefs are preparing food. It's chaotic as we make our way through. We pass through a hall larger than I've ever seen with a winding staircase and a chandelier hanging down. It's more than impressive, and I consider getting out my mobile to snap a few shots so

I can show the girls, but Ella begins to climb the stairs and so I follow eagerly, wanting to see what the bedrooms are like.

ANTON

I pour myself a drink and take a seat. Checking my watch for the hundredth time, I sigh. I hate lateness, and so far, Piper is three minutes late. The sound of heels clicking on the hall floor grabs my attention. Ella appears first in her usual house attire of shorts and an oversized shirt. "Let me present your date for this evening." She smiles wide and steps aside.

Piper steps into the doorway, and I inhale sharply. She looks stunning. Her dress clings to every one of her perfect curves. Her hair is curled and tied to one side so it falls over her shoulder and across her chest. A few loose curls frame her face. Piper doesn't need makeup, but the cost of the makeup artist that Ella insisted on was totally worth it. She looks flawless.

"Thank you, Ella. Please check the guestroom has been made up."

She glances back at Piper before saying, "Actually, Piper isn't staying here this evening."

I smirk, knowing full well Piper *is* spending the evening under this roof because I make the rules. I stand and stride over to the drinks caddy. "Please check on the room, Ella," I repeat as I pour Piper a drink.

I wait for Ella to leave then hold out the wine glass for Piper. She steps closer, taking it. "Anton, I didn't agree to stay over. I'll be going home after dinner."

"I think you're forgetting who holds the power here, Piper. It certainly isn't you." I grin, and she scowls. "My guests will arrive shortly. You should be on your best behaviour tonight."

"If you needed a performing monkey, you should have blackmailed one of those instead."

I run my finger along her jawline, and it sets my skin on fire. "Don't pretend you're not enjoying this. Let's greet my guests."

I hold out my arm, and she stares at it until I raise my brow. She sighs and then hooks her arm into mine. "If we're eating here, why did we bother to dress up?" she asks.

I snigger. She's got a lot to learn about my world and how it's completely different to hers.

Guests have begun to arrive, and I shake hands with them and kiss their wives on the

ANTON

cheek. It's all a show, but I'm used to it as I've been doing this since I was a boy. Eight made men coming together under one roof only happens on rare occasions, but I know there have been whispers about my ability to lead our organisation since I've always been the playboy, along with Tag. All my capos, a couple of them younger than me, are settled down and married. And with my father dying earlier than expected, they've given me time to find my feet, but they need to see I'm taking my role seriously. I'm no longer the playboy of the Mafia—I'm the boss.

"Why aren't Tag and Lucy here?" asks Piper.

"Tag has other business to deal with this evening." The truth is, he hates this sort of thing, and I allowed him to dip out of this one. Now, he owes me a favour, and I plan on taking full advantage of that.

Our waiter for the evening announces dinner is being served, so we make our way through to the dining room. I take the head of the table and nod to my left so Piper understands where she should sit. All the other men take their places, but everyone remains standing until I sit, and then they follow suit.

The waiters bring out the food and begin to serve us. Ella chose the menu. I trust my sister completely to know what will impress people. Apparently, scallops were her choice of starter because the wives would love them. If the wives are happy, then the men usually are, and as I tuck into the delicate seafood, I'm thankful for her help.

"Oh my god," Piper groans around a mouthful of juicy scallop. "These are amazing."

A smile pulls at my lips. "You've never had scallops?" I ask, and she shakes her head before taking another mouthful. I become fixated on her expression, forgetting my own food as she closes her eyes in pleasure and groans again. She swipes her thumb over the corner of her mouth and pops it between her lips to lick it clean.

"That was amazing." She glances at my plate. "Don't you like them?"

I grin, picking up my fork again. "Sorry, I got lost in thought. What about venison? Have you had that?"

Piper thinks for a moment. "I've had a venison burger. Does that count?"

I laugh again and shake my head. "Not really."

ANTON

Matthew, one of the made men, sits to my right, and he leans closer to pull my attention away from Piper. I reluctantly engage in conversation, but my mind is fully on her, and I hardly hear a word he's saying.

I've never been on a dinner date where my date has never eaten this kind of food. And when the venison is placed before her, her eyes widen in delight. She loves food, and it's a refreshing change from the women I usually take out. When she slices her first piece and pops it in her mouth, she looks ready to burst. "Oh, my lord," she says around a mouthful. "This is the best venison I've ever had."

"I thought you'd never had it," I query.

She grins. "Exactly."

"Out of interest, what sort of food do you usually eat?"

"Well, just normal food. Ya know, like pie, chicken." She shrugs her shoulders and scoops a forkful of creamed potato. "Bernie makes a mean chicken and leek pie."

"Sounds delightful," I say, and Piper laughs at my sarcasm.

"You do realise this isn't normal everyday food," she tells me.

"In my world, it is."

She places her fork down and fixes me with a curious stare. "I wonder what you'd make of the real world," she mutters, almost to herself, before picking up her wine and draining the glass.

Chapter Three

♥

PIPER

The food is amazing, better than anything I've ever experienced, and when dessert is served, I laugh. "What's so funny?" asks Anton.

I stare at the small dollop of ice cream with something green sticking out of it. "Ice cream?"

"You don't like ice cream?"

"Sure, it just seems ... dull after all that lovely food."

He smirks. "Taste it, bellissima. My chef's homemade sorbet is a favourite."

I pick off the greenery and hold it up with a raised eyebrow. "And the plant is for?"

He laughs again. "Mint. Mint sorbet served with mint leaf. It's decoration."

"When I have ice cream at home, it's by the tub. You should really think about portion sizes when it comes to stuff like this." I scoop some into my mouth and my tastebuds explode. "Oh, wow," I murmur.

"I told you," Anton says smugly. "Ella chose the menu and she never gets it wrong. After dinner, the men will go off into another room," Anton adds, leaning closer. "I'll introduce you to some of the women."

My eyes widen. "No," I hiss. "Don't you dare leave me."

He pushes away his half-eaten sorbet. "It's how this works, Piper. Relax, they won't bite."

"I don't care. That wasn't the deal. I've had dinner with you, now I should leave."

He arches a brow. "There you go again, thinking you hold all the cards." He then smiles at a woman sitting two seats down from me. "Grace, this is Piper. Take good care of her until I return."

My eyes widen some more as he stands. The rest of the men take his lead and follow like little sheep as he parades them out the room.

The women break out into smaller groups and begin chatting. Grace slides along until she's seated beside me, then she reaches for a bottle of wine from the centre of the table. "Have you and Anton been together long?"

I laugh and shake my head. "God, no. We're not together."

"Oh. Anton gave Carlos the impression you two were a thing. Carlos is my husband."

"This is our first date," I explain, "and far too early to say we're anything at all really, even friends."

"Did the first date go well?" she asks.

I shrug, thinking about the way Anton's forced me into this. "How long have you known him?"

"Since I met Carlos five years ago. He and Carlos have been friends since they were little boys. Tag as well."

"And how many dates has Anton introduced you to?" I ask.

She shifts uncomfortably. "A few," she admits.

I smirk. "Exactly. Let's face it, after tonight, I doubt there will be a follow-up date. It's not his style. But it's been a nice evening and I had some great food, so I can't complain."

It's another hour before the men return. They're laughing, joking, and things seem more relaxed. The guests begin to make their excuses and leave, and when the final couple has left, I finally breathe a sigh of relief. Dinner was nice and all, but I've not felt like myself all evening.

"Drink?" Anton asks, heading over to a small table. He lifts the glass lid off a decanter and begins to pour the contents into a glass.

"No, thank you. I really should be leaving." I yawn and stretch my arms above my head to show him how tired I am. Anton smiles but continues to pour two drinks. He hands me one, and I take it, rolling my eyes. "Why didn't Ella come to dinner this evening?" I ask.

A look passes over Anton's face. I can't quite make it out, but it reminds me of sadness. "She was busy," he eventually says.

"No, she definitely told me that she was bingeing on Netflix tonight."

"Yes, as I said, she was busy. Did you enjoy our date?"

"Dinner was lovely. I'm not sure I fit with your people." I laugh. Anton takes a seat next to me, and I shuffle up to the other end of the couch as discreetly as I can.

"My people?" he repeats.

"Rich. Cultured. Intelligent."

Anton laughs aloud and throws his head back. "Cultured and intelligent? They're merely lucky, and definitely not any of the things you say."

"Lucky in what way?"

Anton thinks about the question. I notice he does that a lot when he wants to find the right answer. He lays his arm along the back of the couch and his fingertips brush my bare shoulder. "Most were born into this world. Like me. We had fathers who were either born into the Mafia or paid their way in. I come from a long line of Italian Mafia, but Tag, for example, his grandfather bought his way in."

"So, Tag is like the third generation of Mafia?"

Anton nods. "It's not all it's cracked up to be," he mutters, swirling his drink around in his glass.

"How does a person buy into the Mafia?" I ask, taking a drink. I wince as it burns its way down my throat. *Christ, it's strong.*

"Are you enquiring for yourself?" he asks, arching a brow.

"I think I'd make a good boss," I joke.

"You pay by earning the respect of the family," he replies.

"That sounds doable. So, it's not really hard to get in. I thought you meant cold hard cash,"

"Respect doesn't come easy, bellissima. It takes dedication, hard work, and a strong stomach. And once you're in, you never get out."

"So, what if Tag tells you he's had enough and wants to ride off into the sunset with Lucy?" I suddenly feel tired, and I pull my legs under me, curling up and getting comfortable.

"It wouldn't happen," he says firmly.

"But if it did?"

"It wouldn't," he replies.

"But if it did?" I push, and Anton looks irritated.

He sighs heavily. "Like I said, he wouldn't be allowed. I would have to stop him."

"How would you stop him?"

He shakes his head in disbelief. "Anyone ever tell you that you ask too many questions?"

I nod. "My mum. I drive her insane with questions. Have ever since I was a little girl." I yawn and lie my head on the back of the couch. "Would you have to stop him, or would you get someone else to do it?"

He stares down at his drink. "I'd do it. I'd have to—it's my role."

"That would be pretty shitty for you both," I surmise, "with you being friends."

"The organisation comes first, over everything."

"Even friends?"

He nods. "Especially friends."

ANTON

It takes almost ten minutes from Piper downing the rest of her drink to her falling into a deep sleep. I thought she'd never stop talking. I prod her shoulder, smiling when she doesn't react at all. I remove my jacket and place it over the back of the couch, and then scoop her sleeping form up into my arms and carry her to bed.

I carefully lay her on the king-sized bed and pull back the sheets. I take a step back. Her dress is beautiful, and she looked absolutely stunning this evening, but I'm pretty sure it isn't comfortable enough to sleep in. I ponder it over for a second, and then I roll her onto her side and unzip the dress from the back. I gently tug it down her body, which isn't easy now she's passed out.

I fold the dress over the back of a nearby chair and glance over her body. Her matching black underwear clings to her tanned skin perfectly.

I go to the bathroom and wet a washcloth, returning to Piper and gently removing all traces of makeup from her face. She doesn't need it, and as I wipe all traces of it away, I realise I prefer her without it.

Covering her over with the sheets, I place a gentle kiss to her forehead. I know she didn't want to stay over, and she'll be raging when she wakes to find herself here, but I had a score to settle with Hulk, and she's the key to that. I open her bag and take out her mobile phone, using her finger to open the screen lock before leaving the room.

When I get into my office, I take her phone apart. I insert a tracking device into the back before putting it all back together and pulling up the tracking app on my own mobile. I make sure I can pick up her signal and smile when it beeps up on my app. *Perfect.*

ANTON

Opening her messages, I see there's one from Lucy asking how the date is going with the 'scum bag'. I laugh to myself. Lucy doesn't hide the fact she dislikes me, and I really don't give a crap. Next is a message from Hulk. It's a photo of Piper half-naked and smiling up at the camera. The text underneath reads, ***Remember this?*** I shake my head. From what Tag told me, he's been treating her like shit for years, which means it's going to be a walk in the park to put my plan into action.

There's a knock on my office door. I glance at the camera and see that it's Michael, so I buzz him in.

"Late night?" I smirk, looking over his blood-stained white shirt. He unbuttons it and rips it from his skin, then goes into the walk-in wardrobe and pulls out a new white shirt.

"Motherfucker bled like a figa."

"Of course he bled like a pussy, that's exactly what he is. *Was*. Why didn't you get one of the runners to do that shit?" I ask, pouring him a whiskey, and he takes it gratefully.

"It needed a personal touch. Badmouthing me is bad enough, but you..." He sighs. "Fucker needed to learn a lesson." One of the soldiers has been getting too big for his boots and bad-mouthing the way we run things. We've made him very rich, letting him build up his own team of runners to sell our product, and it was insulting to know he wasn't grateful.

I watch Michael drink his whiskey. His appearance is very clean cut. He likes to wear suits and expensive ties. His glasses and square jaw give him a model-yet-geeky appearance. You wouldn't expect him to be a brutal, cold-hearted killer. "How did dinner go?"

I smile at the memory of the beautiful girl I have sleeping upstairs. "Good. I've laid the groundwork and now the families think I'm looking to settle down."

Michael nods. "That's good. And the girl is happy with your plan?"

"Not exactly." I pour myself another drink and take a seat at my desk. "I haven't spoken to her about it."

Michael raises his eyebrows. "Okay," he says slowly. "Any reason for that?"

I shake my head. "She isn't exactly weak-willed. It'll take some persuasive talk to get her to agree."

ANTON

Michael sighs and pinches the bridge of his nose. "Why her?"

I laugh and shake my head. "You know I like a challenge, and besides, this is personal."

"Because of the biker?"

"He's been skimming money from me, Michael." He knows this already, but he clearly needs a reminder.

"Talk to Ace. He'll get his men in order."

I shake my head. I trust Ace, but Hulk is his son, and I don't know if they're all in on this. "No. We're doing this my way."

"And Tag doesn't know?" asks Michael. At the mention of Tag, I look away. He's like a brother to me, and I hate keeping this from him, but I know he won't approve of my plan. Tag and I always talked about running things fairly and doing everything differently from how our fathers ran things. It's not as easy as we thought. And now, Tag's married to Hulk's sister, and I don't want him to feel torn. Maybe that's another reason why the guy's so twisted up about the Mafia, because not only do I flirt with his ex, but now his sister is married into it. Either way, I'm taking this personally, and until I know who I can trust, Piper is part of my plan.

Once Michael's left, I head upstairs and look in on Piper. She's exactly how I left her, sound asleep. I smile to myself, wondering how she'll react tomorrow when she realises she's still here and not back at the club like she requested.

I don't get much sleep, but it isn't surprising. I only ever sleep for two or three hours because I have too much shit on my mind to relax. I shower and dress, then head down to the kitchen where Penny is cooking breakfast. She smiles warmly. "Good morning, Mr. Martinez." I nod, taking the newspaper she holds out for me before sitting at the breakfast table. It's the same routine most mornings. "Your mother seems bright today." My smile falters at the mention of her. "She ate some eggs." I pretend to read the newspaper as I can't deal with a conversation about my mother this early in the morning.

Ella waltzes in. "Don't bother to tell him, Penny. He doesn't give a shit."

"Language," I mutter, staring down at the newspaper to avoid the glare I know is directed at me.

ANTON

"How was dinner? I really like Piper." Ella's chirpy tone first thing bugs the shit out of me.

"Don't get too close," I warn. "It's not permanent."

"ANTON!" We all look towards the doorway, where Piper appears looking furious. I lean back, giving her an easy smile. "What the actual fuck?"

"Good morning, Piper. Please, join us for breakfast."

"Fuck you, Anton." She spins on her heel and leaves the room.

Ella exchanges an amused look with Penny, then smirks. "I don't think she's very happy with you."

"No shit," I mutter, throwing down the newspaper and heading after her.

"Language," I hear Ella say as I leave.

Piper's unlocking the front door. She glances back to see me gaining on her and cries out in frustration, working her fingers faster to unfasten the security chains. I reach her, slamming my hand above her head. Her hands fall to her sides. "Let's not start the day on bad terms," I whisper in her ear. "If I'm in a bad mood, it affects everyone around me."

"Did you drug me?" she snaps, turning to face me and realising what a mistake that is when we're so close. Still, she squares her shoulders and glares at me, waiting for my response.

"He's obsessed," I say, and she frowns. I pull her mobile phone from my pocket, and her eyes widen.

"You took my phone?"

"Nonstop messages," I continue, flicking through the messages from Hulk. "And you were only gone a night. Do you see how this could work for you?"

"What are you talking about?"

"Does he always message you, or is it because he knew you were with me?" She shrugs. "I'm betting the latter."

"What do you want from me, Anton?" she cries.

"All we have to do is pretend to be fucking." I move my mouth to her ear. "It could work for both of us."

"Why?" she asks. "Why do you want me to agree to this?"

"I have my reasons."

"Which are?" she demands.

ANTON

I grin, moving my lips just a breath from hers. She inhales sharply, and her tongue darts out to wet her lower lip. "None of your business." I push off from the door and head back to the kitchen. "Now, let's eat. I'm hungry."

"Anton," she hisses. I ignore her, knowing she'll follow because she wants the attention from Hulk and I've just offered it on a plate.

Chapter Four

PIPER

I endure an uncomfortably silent breakfast with Anton and Ella. He insists I eat, even when I tell him I'm not hungry, and he stares down at the newspaper the entire time, only glancing up to ensure I'm eating.

Then he insists on dropping me home on his way to the office, which only drags out the uncomfortable feeling I have in the pit of my stomach. I'm pretty sure he gave me sleeping pills or something last night, and his confusing statement about us dating only messed with my already foggy head. What would he possibly get out of it if I were to agree? It's not like he can't get any woman he wants.

ANTON

I get tired of the silence, so I let out a loud sigh before glancing his way. He's staring intently at his mobile phone. "What exactly would it entail?" I ask.

Anton looks up. "What?"

I glance at his driver, hoping to God he can't hear me. "What you said this morning," I hiss.

I feel like he enjoys my discomfort as he glances at the driver also before smirking. "It would entail us acting like a couple. Dating, spending time together . . . whatever couples do."

I arch an eyebrow at him. "The couples that I know have sex."

"You want to have sex with me?" he asks, now fully grinning.

I feel my cheeks redden. "No!" I screech. "This whole thing's weird. I don't know what you want from me."

He exhales, tucking his mobile away. "Piper, it's not that complicated."

The car slows and I look out the window to see we're not at the clubhouse. Instead, we're at the gates of a house the size of a mansion. It looks like some kind of country club only . . . not in the country.

I sit up straighter. "Why are we here? I thought you were taking me home."

"It's just a quick pit-stop. There's an issue I need to deal with."

The driver steps out and opens my door. I look back to find Anton already out the car and rounding my side. "I'll wait here," I tell him.

"You'll follow me."

I roll my eyes and get out to follow. He's so damn bossy, maybe that's why he can't find a real date. "What is this place?"

"It's one of my private clubs. I co-own it, but my partner is on holiday at the moment."

As soon as we step inside, it's obvious this place is way out of my league. Everything inside the place looks expensive, from the white and grey marble floors to the crystal chandeliers. In front of us is a huge lobby with a female standing behind a welcome desk. She smiles brightly, showing us her white teeth. "Good morning, Mr. Martinez. Mr. Griar is waiting in your office."

Anton nods in acknowledgment and then turns to look at me. "There's a lounge area just through—" He's cut off when shouting erupts from the elevator. A man steps out, looking

ANTON

pissed, and a female dressed in next to nothing follows him.

"That was not part of the plan and you know it," the woman yells.

"I want to speak to—" the man begins but stops when he spots Anton. "Ah, Mr. Martinez, just the person." He holds out his hand for Anton to shake, but Anton just stares down at it like it's diseased. The man looks taken aback but seems to think better of calling Anton out and withdraws his hand. "This whore was—"

Anton moves fast, stepping closer to the man and taking him by surprise. He's so close, it's intimidating. "Stop talking." His voice is dangerously low, and I feel my skin prickle as a large man appears behind Anton. He's tall as well as wide, and I can only assume he's some kind of security.

"Can I help, Mr. Martinez?" he asks.

"I have a problem I need to deal with in my office, Damon. Please take Mr. Cramner to one of the meeting rooms." Anton then turns to the woman and takes her hand gently. "Are you okay, Maisy?" She nods. "Good. Can you take my guest to the lounge and then take the rest of the day off? Full pay, of course."

She nods and kisses his cheek. "Thank you, Mr. Martinez. I appreciate that."

"Full pay? Are you crazy? She's a fucking . . ." the man begins. I don't hear him finish the sentence because he is abruptly escorted from the reception area by Damon.

Maisy smiles. "This way," she tells me, leading us to another room. "Take a seat. Help yourself to whatever you want," she adds as I take in my lavish surroundings. "Please don't leave this room without Mr. Martinez. He doesn't like people wandering around here."

"What kind of place is this?" I ask.

"If you don't know, it's because he doesn't want you to."

I take a seat. Anton's got so many shady businesses, I'm not surprised she wasn't willing to explain. And like so many of his other places, this one screams wealth and exclusivity. Which brings me back to the same question—what in the hell does he want with me? Places like this come with women. His lifestyle comes with women. It makes no sense unless it's purely to piss off Hulk. With Anton being in such a high position, would he be so childish? I guess he's known for his games, since it's how Tag met Lucy.

I sigh heavily and once again glance around the room. Why does he bring me to these places if he doesn't want me to know his business? My patience was never very long, so I stand and wander over to a door at the far side of the room, placing my hand on the large golden handle. Carefully, I twist until it pops open and then I wait for a beat, just in case Anton is on the other side of it. When nothing happens, I slowly pull it open to find another lounge-like area but on a smaller scale. I walk through and open the next door, this time finding myself in a lobby with a winding staircase. There's no one around, so I proceed to climb the stairs to the next floor. There are offices all along the corridor containing large tables surrounded by chairs, the types you'd find in meeting rooms, but they're all empty.

At the end of the hallway, there's a door which is propped open. As I get closer, I see it's another office. A large oak desk sits in front of a window, similar to Anton's office. I hear a door bang farther down the hallway and panic, gently pushing the door to. I peer through the window, which looks down onto the grounds. Anton's car is waiting out front, and Michael is leaning against it, chatting into his mobile and smoking a cigarette.

I'm about to turn to leave when hands grip my hair, yanking my head back. I yelp in surprise and automatically raise my hands to try and free myself. My wrists are taken and pulled behind my back, and I realise it's not Anton as I'm pushed to the desk and forced to bend over it.

"What the fuck?" I snap, kicking out my legs.

"You kept us waiting," a voice hisses in my ear. Metal cuffs are placed on one wrist and then the other. "We hate waiting."

I twist, but the man pushes his weight against me, forcing me to lie flat. "There's been some kind of mistake," I tell him. Another man steps into my view, grinning as he unfastens his belt, and it dawns on me that I'm in real danger. My breath sticks in my throat, making it hard for any words to escape, and I try hard to inhale air into my tight lungs. The man takes some of his weight from me and gropes my arse.

"The only mistake is that you didn't come dressed as I ordered," he replies, grinding against my backside.

I screw my eyes shut. "You don't understand. I'm here with Anton."

His friend grins, wiping his thumb across my lower lip. "You think name dropping will get you out of here?"

"You don't understand—"

The door opens, slamming against the wall, and fear envelopes me at the thought of more men. "You better fucking explain yourself real quick before I blow your brains all over this place." I sob with relief at the sound of Anton's voice, my entire body sagging.

The man's weight leaves my body. "What the hell?" he snaps. "We're in the middle of roleplay."

"Roleplay with my fucking guest?" yells Anton, and I hear a thud and then a grunt. I'm guided to stand, and then I'm turned in Michael's arms. He looks me up and down with concern, like he's surveying me for damage. I look to the two men and see Anton has one by the throat against the wall. In his other hand is his gun, and it's pressed firmly against the man's head.

"She's good, Anton," Michael confirms, and he nods at me, urging me to confirm it.

"I'm fine. It took me by surprise," I mutter. My voice is shaky and unlike me, and I cough to clear it. "It was obviously a misunderstanding."

"Get her out of here, Michael," Anton orders. He thrusts a set of handcuff keys towards Michael as I'm guided from the room.

I'm taken to an office just a few rooms away from where I was moments ago. This one is bright and furnished well, with leather chairs and full bookshelves.

"Why were you up here?" asks Michael, unfastening the handcuffs.

I rub my wrists. "I was bored waiting, so I went to see what this place was all about." Michael shakes his head, laughs to himself, and then leaves. I wrap my arms around myself and take a few calming breaths. The door opens and Anton glares at me. His shoulders are hunched forwards, and he's breathing heavy.

"What the fuck were you doing up here?" he demands.

"I was looking for you," I lie.

"You were told to stay in that room," he growls.

I shrug my shoulders. "I'm not very good at doing as I'm told."

"They thought you were up for that. They thought you were one of the girls."

I stare at him blankly, waiting for him to explain further, but he doesn't bother to. Instead, he stalks over to a small table that has a drink decanter on, tips some of the amber liquid into a crystal glass and swirls it. I glance at my watch. "A little early for that," I mutter, and he scowls in my direction. "What did they think I was up for anyway?"

"Nothing, forget about it. Are you okay?"

"Now you ask me if I'm okay?" I mumble. "Is that what happens here? You wander into rooms and get attacked? Are the girls up for that?"

"You shouldn't have left the lounge," he repeats.

"You shouldn't have brought me here," I counter. "You have dangerous men attacking women and you thought it would be a good idea to leave me alone? This is your fault, Anton, not mine."

He mutters something under his breath and pulls out his mobile. He shoots off a quick text before stuffing it back in his pocket and turning away from me to look out the window.

A minute later, there's a knock at the door and Michael enters. He looks back and forth between us, and when neither of us speaks, he eventually smiles at me stiffly. "Come with me. I'll drop you home."

I glare at the back of Anton's head. "That's it? You're sending me home with your driver?"

"Go home, Piper." His voice is firm and disinterested, which only furthers my rage.

"I thought we had a deal?" I ask, trying anything to get him to look at me. It doesn't work.

"The deal is off the table. It won't work." He turns around but ignores me and looks to Michael. "Please collect Melissa after you've dropped Piper home. We're moving to plan B."

ANTON

Plan B. I don't have a plan B. I didn't have a plan A until Piper danced on my club stage. Nevertheless, Michael nods like he knows exactly what I'm talking about and tries to usher Piper towards the door. "Who the hell is Melissa?" she asks. Melissa is a hook-up. One that I've not seen in months, which reminds me, I must text Michael and make sure he doesn't actually go and collect her. She's the last thing I need.

I roll my eyes and head for the door. Piper can't follow simple instructions, so she's no use to me and the sooner she gets the message, the better. I'll find another way to get to Hulk.

She follows me along the hallway. "I don't understand why you're so mad with me when I was the one who got attacked."

"You were attacked because you can't follow simple instructions." I continue to walk away, taking long strides in the hope she'll get bored and let Michael escort her home.

"You didn't tell me not to leave the room, those words did not leave you mouth."

"But you knew not to leave," I say coldly. The fact she almost got hurt chills me. How can I keep her safe in my world when she doesn't listen? Those idiots thought she was roleplaying, pretending she wasn't up for it. They'd have forced themselves upon her and it would have been my fault. My life is too chaotic to involve a woman.

She continues to follow me down the stairs. I go through the door behind the reception desk, which leads down to the soundproof basement. It's just one of the many soundproof rooms I have. "Where are you going?" she asks.

I stop at the foot of the stairs and flick the light on. The room is suddenly bathed in fluorescent white light and in the centre sits Ivan. He holds a high membership at this club. One that allows him access to our roleplay rooms. But with that comes rules, and by groping Piper in that office today, he broke them because he knows he should've had a code word for that type of roleplay. His eyes fix on me, and I see the fear that he's trying so hard to hide. He's a cockroach. Any man who gets off by forcing women, roleplay or not, is a cockroach.

My business partner in this club, Andrew, would argue it's better he does it here with willing women than out on the streets, but I don't agree.

"Ivan, we meet again." I smile, and he stands. He thinks that by hiding his fear, I'll be impressed, but I'm not. It pisses me off more. "Sit down." The order is firm, and he adheres without argument. "Apologise to my guest."

ANTON

"Why was she allowed to wander around like that, Anton?" he asks, suddenly sounding angry. I land the first punch squarely on his chiselled jaw, and he hisses, shaking his head.

I lean close to his ear. "You're forgetting your manners, Ivan," I whisper. I brush off his jacket and firmly press down on his shoulders. "Now, let's try again. Apologise to my guest."

Piper squares her shoulders and folds her arms over her chest. She doesn't look scared, and I wonder how much violence she's previously been exposed to in that damn club.

"I'm sorry," mumbles Ivan.

"It's pretty sick, yah know," says Piper, and I stifle my smirk as she steps closer. I like her balls. "You get a kick out of forcing a woman. You should really see someone about that."

Ivan shrugs off my hands from his shoulders. "Fuck you," he spits. "I'm not going to sit here and let some bitch talk down to me. Cunts like you are good for nothing but fucking. Trust me, I smell it a mile off."

My hands are squeezing his neck before I'm even aware that I've reacted. He clutches desperately at my hands, trying to free himself. "Sweetheart, I felt your erection against my backside, and trust me when I say it would take more than that tiny dick to get me off." I watch in awe as Piper turns and heads up the stairs. I'm so busy staring after her that I don't notice Ivan is now slumped and I'm holding him up by his neck. He's passed out, so I drop him to the floor and pull out my handkerchief to wipe my hands. I step over him and follow after Piper, reaching her as she's passing the reception desk.

"Stop," I bark, but she continues towards the exit. I have an urge to keep her here and, without thinking, I scoop her up and throw her over my shoulder. She yelps, hitting me on the back, but I take no notice as I head for the stairs. The receptionist stares in surprise. My staff never see me behave like this, especially not with a woman. I take the stairs two at a time and stride towards my office, where I shove the door open, letting it slam back against the wall. Michael looks up from behind my desk and smirks. He rises to his feet and, as he passes to leave, he pats me on the shoulder.

I lock the door and place Piper on her feet. Her hair covers her face in messy strands, and as I push my hands in it to clear it away, I feel

ANTON

it tangle around my fingers. Her tanned cheeks are flushed, and her breathing is rapid, much like my own. I back her to the wall, and she gasps. It's such a small intake of breath, but I hear it and know without a doubt that I want to make her gasp more.

I tentatively move my face closer and, when she doesn't immediately shove me away, I allow my lips to brush hers. I tug gently on the roots of her hair, and when she gasps again, I take advantage of her open mouth and take the kiss deeper, swiping my tongue against hers in a hungry battle. The control I always have is slipping away, and it's replaced with a burning desire to have her right now. Our mouths begin to mash together, like we're desperately searching for something that will keep this feeling alive. I don't understand the reaction that my body's having to her, but I'm reluctant to let it go.

My hands move of their own accord, traveling hungrily down her body. Gripping the hem of her top, I tug it up and she puts her hands in the air, allowing me to remove it. Our mouths clash together again, and she feels her way to the buttons of my crisp white shirt. Once she gets it open, she pushes her hands up my stomach and over my chest. Her nails carefully rake over my taut skin, and it sends shivers down my spine. Somewhere in the back of my mind, I know this is taking the plan too far, too soon. But I can't stop.

I'm addicted.

Chapter Five

PIPER

Sleeping with the Mafia boss was not on my to-do list . . . until now. The way his eyes burn into me like he wants to eat me alive sets me on fire. I need to have him . . . now.

There's no hesitation as Anton's hand pushes into my knickers and roughly swipes through my wetness. I shudder, slamming my palms against his hard chest. *Fuck, it feels good.* I close my eyes and slide my hands to his shoulders, digging my nails into his skin as he moves his fingers against my clit. My toes curl tightly as a tingling feeling burns through my body. It becomes too much, and as I begin to quiver under his expert touch, he stops. "What are you stopping for?" I pant.

"My mobile," he mutters. "It's buzzing." He withdraws his hand, and I almost cry out at the loss.

"Are you kidding me right now? Ignore it," I practically wail.

Instead, Anton pulls the mobile from his pocket and presses it to his ear. "Hulk, this better be good. I'm in the middle of something." He listens for a second and then disconnects the call. "Get dressed. We have to go."

"But we—" Anton cuts me off by thrusting my top at me.

"Ace and Mae are home," he states, and my head spins.

It hits me hard. I haven't thought about Mae since I opened my eyes this morning. I've been so wrapped up in Anton that I've forgotten the complete misery that Mae has been faced with. Shame dampens my sexual appetite, and I dress rapidly as Anton does the same.

Michael manoeuvres expertly through the busy London streets. I sit in the back next

ANTON

to Anton, who's staring intently at his mobile. Maybe the interruption was a good thing. I have enough complications in my life without adding to them.

We arrive and the clubhouse is busy. The feeling of elation bounces around amongst the members because not only is their President home, but so is Bernie's daughter. Everyone loves Mae like their own.

When I finally spot her pale and tired face, I burst into tears. The days since she's been gone have been harder than I realised, and I'm weighed down with the fear of what could have been. I can't get to her because she's too wrapped up in everyone else's arms, so I watch from a distance, crying into my sleeve. I feel arms snake around my waist from behind, and for a split second, I'm disappointed when I realise it's Hulk and not Anton.

"I thought we were never going to see them again," he whispers close to my ear. I nod in agreement. We all thought the same when we received no ransom or threats.

"They look washed out," I mutter. "Do we know where they've been?"

Hulk snuggles his face into my hair and takes a deep breath. "No. I haven't managed to speak to him properly yet, but I will. And when I find out, I'm gonna blow that place up and kill every fucker in it."

"Good," I whisper, wiping my eyes. Whoever took Ace and Mae deserve to die.

Hulk turns me in his arms, and I press my cheek against his chest. It seems so natural for us to be like this, which makes it all the harder to accept every time he pushes me away. My eyes lock onto the dark, burning globes of Anton's eyes. He's staring so intently from across the room that my heart beats wildly in my chest. *Why do I feel like I'm doing something wrong?* I take a step back from Hulk. "I'd better push my way in there to see Mae or I'll be waiting hours." I smile. "Look, Hulk, I'm really sorry for putting you through so much shit these last few days. I've been worried about Mae, and it's made me do some stupid shit."

Hulk reaches out, cupping my face in his large hands. He uses his thumbs to wipe away the tear tracks that undoubtedly stain my skin. "Your fire and rebellious streak are just some of the reasons that I—" he begins to say but is

ANTON

abruptly cut off when I'm hit hard from behind and enveloped in Mae's arms.

"I've missed you so much," she cries. I hold her arms against my chest and smile through the tears that fall again.

"Oh, you have no idea, Mae," I sob. "Don't you ever get yourself kidnapped ever again," I add, and she laughs.

We don't get any chance to catch up properly before Mae is whisked away again. The men have been called into church, and Anton and Tag are hanging back, waiting to be called in. I sit on one of the couches in the main room and watch my mum and Bernie fuss around Mae. She'll never be allowed out of their sight again. The space next to me dips as Anton lowers himself into the spot.

"What the fuck was that earlier with Hulk?" he asks.

"We got caught in a moment," I mutter. "Happy to have his dad and my best friend home."

"If we're sticking to some kind of plan, it's best you don't melt at his every fucking touch," he says quietly but with as much venom as if he was shouting in my face. "Act like you're my queen and he'll be eating out of your hand forever. You roll back into bed with him, then he'll be back to using you within the day."

"I thought our deal was off," I reply.

"That was until I touched you. The deal is back on, and we play it my way."

I stare down at my fingers as I knot them together. "Yah know, he's not as bad as you think. He can be kind and sweet."

He scoffs, rolling his eyes. "Did you see the woman that Ace brought back with him? Hulk couldn't keep his eyes off her arse. He's a player, Piper, and if you want him eating out your hand, listen to me."

I glance at the tall blonde that came back with Ace and Mae. She's pretty, and I can imagine that she's Hulks type. "I didn't actually agree to take part in the plan."

"You almost came on my hand, Piper, wasn't that your agreement?"

I feel a blush creep across my cheeks. "I was caught in the moment."

"And now you want Hulk to finish what I started?" he quips, smirking.

"No," I say defensively.

"Then we're agreed. Your first job is tonight. I need you to attend a charity function with me.

I'll have a dress sent over." I open my mouth to protest, but Anton leans forward and plants another one of his toe-curling kisses on me. It's so unexpected that I feel myself relax against him, completely wrapped up in the moment. When he pulls back and winks, I see mischief behind the smile. When he stands, I see Hulk waiting in the doorway for church. He's staring directly at me with a pissed expression, and my heart immediately aches. "We'll finish what we started tonight," Anton throws back over his shoulder as he passes Hulk.

ANTON

I straighten the black bow tie sitting neatly at my throat. "I don't fucking buy it," Tag snaps angrily. "Why Piper? Hulk's my brother-in-law, and he and Piper just have a weird relationship. Leave them to it."

"He treats her like crap," I remind him.

"Since when do you give a shit about women?" he asks. "Lucy isn't happy about any of this and she's on my back about it."

"Is Lucy ever happy, Tag?" I ask on a sigh. "Stop worrying. I like her, okay?"

He frowns. "There're women lining up to date you, choose one of them. Piper doesn't deserve to get hurt by you."

"You sound like a whiny bitch. You're spending too much time with Lucy."

"Don't push me, man," he mutters.

I turn to face him. I give him my most sincere look and hope it's enough to convince him. "I like her. She's a little crazy. She outright questions everything I do or say, and you don't get that kind of defiance in a woman these days. I like it. It started as a little fun. Maybe the blackmail side of it was what lured me to her, but now, well . . ." I shrug my shoulders and leave the sentence open.

"That's exactly what scares me, Anton. She's defiant. She's a liability at the best of times. What if she sees something she shouldn't? What if you put her at risk? I feel like something bad is just waiting to happen."

I'm annoyed by his judgmental tone. All the fears that I keep to myself about dating have just been laid out there by my best friend and it pisses me off. "So, what, am I not supposed to ever be happy? Most of the men in this family are married, but me. Without marriage, the men will never truly relax under me. They'll question whether I can lead without producing an heir. Is that what you want?" I pull on my dinner jacket and run my fingers through my hair. "Maybe it is. Maybe you want to stand here instead of me." I regret the words the instant they leave my mouth, and I see the hurt on Tag's face, which only makes me feel worse.

"Fuck you, Anton. Fuck you." He heads for the door, and I groan aloud. He's always supported me. To throw that accusation in his face was a low blow, even for me.

"Watch yourself," I yell after him. He might be my closest friend, but I'm his boss at the end of the day, and he can't be overheard speaking to me like that.

By the time I make my way downstairs, Ella is waiting with my glass of bourbon and the necklace I asked her to collect on my behalf. She gives me a crooked smile. "You scrub up okay for an arse."

I take the jewellery box from her and open it. The crystals blink at me in the harsh lighting of the kitchen. Piper will hate it, but it'll go lovely with her dress. "Are you sure you won't come?" I ask again, and Ella shakes her head. Since everything came out about our father and the abuse she suffered, she's taken a back seat in everything social. It saddens me because she used to be a social butterfly.

"Someone has to sit with Mum," she says brightly, and I know it's a little dig at the fact I haven't been in to see her today.

"El, I'll see her tomorrow. And you don't need to sit with her. I pay the staff to do that."

"Tag sat with her today," she says. I sigh and give her a look that warns her to stop talking. She holds her hands up. "Fine. I'll tell her you'll be in tomorrow."

Michael is the driver tonight, mainly because I trust him over everyone, and with Tag's dad still running around like a lunatic, I don't want to take unnecessary risks by having someone with me who can't shoot straight. He stops the Bentley outside the clubhouse, where Piper is waiting by the roadside. I frown. She's a target out here like this. Someone should be with her. As she settles in the back seat beside me, I ask, "Why are you waiting out here?"

"Hulk was giving me a hard time. I had to get out of there."

ANTON

"You shouldn't be out alone, Piper. Next time, call me. I'll come quicker." She nods, but the sad expression on her face remains. "I got you a present." I hold out the black box, and she takes it.

"Why?"

I shrug. "Because that's what people do when they're in a relationship."

"How would you know?" she asks with a smirk.

"Tag told me." Her smile fades again. "Aw, don't tell me. You've had a lecture from Lucy?" She nods in response. "She'll get over it. We just need to ride the storm."

Piper opens the box and gasps. That sound stirs all kinds of heat inside me, and I clench my fists to get control of myself again. "Anton, this is way too much. I can't accept it."

"It goes with the dress. If you don't accept it, I'll be offended. Michael, what happens when I get offended?" I ask, keeping my tone light-hearted, so she knows I'm kidding.

"Oh, you really don't want to know," he quips, catching my eye in the rear-view mirror. I take the delicate piece from the box and unfasten the clasp. She leans closer so I can place it around her neck. The crystals go perfectly with the silk grey evening dress that I'd sent over to Piper earlier. With her hair up and just the odd tendril framing her face, she looks amazing. Far from the biker chick I usually see wearing joggers or denim cut-offs.

We arrive at the hotel. Tonight's event is being hosted by the mayor of London. Rubbing shoulders with politicians is a large part of my job. Without them, I wouldn't be able to get away with half the underground shit that I do, and without me, they wouldn't be able to control the crime. I shake hands with various business types as we move through to the main room. I spot Tag and Lucy and, knowing that Piper will feel more comfortable around Lucy, I steer us over to them. Shaking hands with Tag, who reluctantly participates, I lean in towards him. "Sorry. I shouldn't have said that. I know it's not true."

"Damn right, it's not true, Anton. You're getting paranoid."

ANTON

"Let me make it up to you. What are you drinking?"

Tag rolls his eyes. "Shut the hell up, man. I can buy my own drinks. I'll beat your arse down at the gym tomorrow, bright and early." I nod in agreement. All our disputes are settled in the gym. Turning to Lucy, I smile, and she scowls. I actually enjoy our love-hate relationship, and I think she feels the same. I lean down and kiss her on each cheek.

"You look amazing, Lucy, as always."

"Good enough to live up to my reputations as a whiny bitch?" she quips, raising a perfectly plucked brow. I glance at Tag and see him laughing.

"You told her I said that?" I ask, and he laughs harder. "Some things should not be shared."

Tag and Lucy are distracted by a passing couple, so I turn to Piper and see she still looks upset. It shouldn't bother me, but it does. The fact that she's thinking about Hulk while she's with me pisses me off. "Everything okay?" I ask.

"I'm tired."

I take two glasses of Champagne from a passing waitress and hand one to Piper. "I'm sure it's not often you get taken to such lavish events. Make the most of it."

"Before you get bored and move on to someone else?"

I carefully consider her choice of words before replying. It almost sounds like she thinks we're a real couple. "Is that what Hulk said, or Lucy?"

"It's a fact, isn't it? Why exactly do you want to pretend to date me? What are you getting out of it?"

"Apart from the fact I get to enjoy your excellent company at these events?" I ask dryly. "It's not your concern. All you need to know is we're both getting something out of it."

"Are you using me?" she asks bluntly.

"Yes." She looks taken aback by my honest answer, but I'm not sure what she expected me to say. We're using each other, and I made that perfectly clear. Lucy re-joins us. "I'll let you ladies catch up. I have some business to attend to." I place a chaste kiss on Piper's head before heading towards the mayor.

Chapter Six

PIPER

Lucy clinks her glass against mine. "To Mafia husbands," she says sarcastically.

I sigh. "What's the big deal, Lucy?" She gave me a strong text lecture earlier when I'd told her that I'd enjoyed my date with Anton. "This is the second date. I'm hardly marching up the aisle with him." I should tell her that it's not real, that we're using one another, but I know it'll only make her worse.

"Because I know him, Piper. Two dates for a man who never dates is suspicious. If he falls for you, do you think you'll be able to walk away? Do you think he'll let you?"

"Yes. He's hardly going to slit my throat if I decide not to date him anymore."

"I wouldn't bet on it. What about Hulk? Last week, you said you loved him, and now, here you are with Anton."

"That's unfair. You know how Hulk's treated me, Lucy. Am I supposed to wait around and hope he falls in love with me too?"

"Hulk doesn't know how to explain how he feels. We all know he loves you."

I press my lips together in a hard line. I've heard this same bullshit from numerous friends about Hulk, and I'm so fed up with hearing it. "I'd believe that, Lucy, if he wasn't sleeping with every female who bats her eyelashes in his direction. He's a womaniser and a possible sex addict. I'm tired of having my heart broken over and over. When Mae and Ace returned, they brought back a woman who helped them. She's stunning. She had every man staring at her, including your brother. The only man who didn't pay her an ounce of attention was Anton. Maybe it's nice to have a man who looks at me like I'm worth it."

I don't give Lucy a chance to respond. I lift the hem of my dress slightly and leave the room. It's been an emotional day and I'm exhausted. I

ANTON

can feel tears threatening to fall, so I follow the signs for the bathroom.

Luckily, it's empty. I drain my glass of Champagne and place it on the sink unit. Resting my hands against it, I stare at myself in the mirror. I don't look like myself. My makeup is sophisticated. I made sure to apply it so that I would fit into Anton's world, yet somehow, I still feel like a fraud. "What am I doing?" I mutter to myself, and then I cry. I let the tears flow freely. For Mae and the things she's been through, and for me and my aching heart. I'm not sure how long I stand there on my own crying, but when the door opens, I straighten my posture and use my hands to pat my cheeks dry.

A handkerchief is dangled before my face, and I groan at the sight of Anton in the reflection of the mirror. I take the hanky and wipe my eyes. My face is a red, blotchy mess, and my eyes are swollen. "Sorry about this," I sniffle, forcing myself to smile.

"Don't be. It's been a rough day. How is Mae?"

I shrug my shoulders. "Not good. She didn't go into too much detail, but I can imagine the stuff she's been through."

"We'll get the people responsible, Piper. I promise you." I know he's telling the truth. His eyes burn with promise. "I shouldn't have forced you to come tonight."

"Nonsense. Give me a minute, I'll pull myself together, and we can go and eat dinner." He nods and leaves me alone.

When I step from the bathroom, Anton is waiting for me. He takes me by the hand and leads me to the elevator. "Where are we going?" I ask, glancing back at the bustling room.

"Well, you clearly aren't in the right frame of mind to be social this evening," he says, giving my hand a gentle squeeze. "So, I thought we could have dinner alone. Just the two of us." My heart swells at his thoughtful gesture. It's hard to remember the reason I'm here when he's acting so sweet.

At the top floor, he leads me to one of the three doors on the landing. He sticks a key card into the first door, and it flashes green before clicking open. The room inside is beautiful, but I'm aware this is a hotel room and I panic at the thought of Anton bringing me up here to finish what we started earlier. He seems to sense my

ANTON

inner turmoil and is quick to lead me past the bedroom, straight out onto the balcony.

I gasp at the scene before me. Laid out beautifully is a table set for two with a flickering candle in the centre. "I didn't want you to miss out on the dinner," he explains, whipping the silver dome from one of the plates. "Lobster."

I smile. "You have a fascination with feeding me."

"I was shocked at dinner last night when you hadn't tried some of those foods. I'm excited to see what you think of lobster."

I take the seat that Anton pulls out for me. He places a napkin across my lap and takes his own seat. Even though we're in central London and I can hear the traffic below, it still feels magical. The skyline is glowing with the city street lights, and I'm reminded of why I love this place so much. "If you eat this sort of stuff all the time, have you ever eaten a hamburger or..." I pause to think. "A hotdog?" Anton screws his face up, and I laugh. "You've never? Have you had McDonald's?"

"No. I've always had cooks who source the best meat, fish, and vegetables, and I eat what they cook. I have no need to get takeout or eat junk food."

I taste a forkful of the juicy white lobster meat and groan with pleasure. "Mmm, this is good," I say. "But I'm taking you to get a burger sometime."

"If I get food poisoning, then it'll be your fault."

"I've never had food poisoning yet, and trust me when I say, I've eaten from street vendors that would make a rat's kitchen look clean." Anton shudders. "Do you always wear suits?" I ask. "Don't you ever slip into joggers and just kick back and relax?"

Anton laughs. "Kick back and relax?" he repeats. "These days, I wouldn't know what that was." He seems to get lost in thought for a few moments before clearing his throat. "I don't get much time to relax. This is one of the reasons I asked you to consider the plan. I don't have time for a girlfriend who wants to go on real dates and kick back and relax."

"Everything's about business," I say. "Isn't that a little boring?"

He laughs again and raises his eyebrows. "It's my life. People are depending on me to play a role."

"Your mum and sister?" I ask.

At the mention of his mum, he winces slightly. "Not just them. I was born to be exactly who I am."

I sip my white wine. It's crisp against the buttery taste of the lobster. "If somebody is born into something, then it isn't their personal choice. If you had a choice, would you choose this?"

He sighs and pushes his untouched plate away. "What about you? What do you do with your time?"

"You don't like answering questions," I point out.

"You ask a lot. What do club princesses do all day? Sit with the big, strong bikers and giggle at their jokes?"

I bite my inner cheek to stop from smiling. "Actually, the club whores are the ego boosters. I have a little more stature around the club."

"Oh. Because I heard women weren't club members unless they became old ladies themselves. I assumed that's why you were so dead set on caging Hulk."

Maybe I dented his ego when I asked the questions I did, but he's being intentionally annoying to get a rise from me, and so I lean back in my chair and fix him with my best poker face. "I want to cage Hulk because he's good in bed."

Anton smirks and takes a drink of his bourbon. "Just *good*? So, you'd spend the rest of your life chained to a man who's just *good* in bed?"

"Why don't you wanna talk about your mum?" I ask, my tone antagonistic.

"What makes him good? And what does he need to do to be upgraded to amazing?"

I stand and move over to the guardrail, looking down at the busy street below. We're so high that the people rushing around look like ants. "Is your relationship strained? Perhaps you blame her for this role you're in when it's not what you want."

Anton rushes me from behind and pins me hard against the rail. I inhale sharply as the air is knocked from my lungs. "Make no mistake, Piper. I'm a good capo. I enjoy what I do. I don't answer questions because it's none of your business. You're not my woman, and even if you were, you'd have to be a pretty good lay before I started telling you bedtime stories about my relationship with my mother."

My breathing comes in short bursts. I'm not sure if I'm still in shock or turned-on. My hands grip tightly onto the rail, turning my knuckles white, just in case he has any crazy thoughts of tipping me over the edge. "It's a real shame," he whispers, carefully running a finger over my cheek.

"What is?"

"That you'll only ever know what *good* is like. I could show you amazing." He sighs and then steps away from me and disappears back into the room. I wipe my sweating hands on a napkin and take a deep, shaky breath. Something about Anton lures me in, even though I know I shouldn't go there.

I feel like Beauty, compelled to follow the beast and rescue him. It's a dangerous game that thrills me as much as it excites me.

ANTON

I sit on the edge of the king-sized bed and pull out my mobile. I need business to take my mind off this woman who is somehow getting inside my head. She asks too many questions, and the scary thing is, I want to answer every one of them. I want to confess that I can't look at my mother because she's playing the victim when it was Ella who suffered. I want to tell her that I hate my mother for sitting in her bedroom day after day, staring out the window, refusing to speak to anyone.

Deep down, I know she misses him. She misses the man who preferred to have sex with his young daughter over her, and I wonder if that makes her jealous. Jealous over her innocent daughter who kept his secret to stop our family falling apart. I shake the thoughts from my mind and open the emails on my phone.

Minutes later, I feel Piper step into the room. I continue to scroll through my emails, not actually reading any of them. "I was about thirteen years old when I first thought about Hulk in that way. Mae and I were sitting out back of the clubhouse sunbathing, and he was out there fixing up an old bike. One of the club whores was pawing all over him and it pissed me off. From that day forward, I never really looked at anyone else."

ANTON

I'm not interested in the love story of Piper and Hulk, but I want to hear her voice, so I tuck my mobile away and ask, "Did you tell him?"

She smiles and jumps onto the bed. She sits dead in the centre and folds her legs, and it reminds me of how teachers used to make us sit at school. "Yes. Well, Mae did. Typical teenage girl style. She marched right up to him and said, 'Piper fancies you,' and he laughed."

I shake off my suit jacket and throw it over to the chair. "Why'd he laugh?"

"He said I was a kid. There wasn't much of an age gap, but being a teenage boy in an MC is the same as being a man. He was already having sex with just about every club girl, and there was no way I was gonna have sex with him at thirteen."

I smirk. "You were a good girl?" I ask with doubt lacing my words.

Piper holds her hand to her chest. "Of course," she says defensively. "I had all kinds of ideas about being a virgin bride. I wanted to wait until my wedding night, and I wanted rose petals on the bed and candles everywhere." Her face falls serious. "I had it all planned out."

"So, what happened? Cos, if you tell me you're still a virgin, I'm taking you to the chapel right now and we're marrying." I laugh, and she smiles.

"On my sixteenth birthday, Hulk convinced me to have sex with him." She doesn't look happy when she tells me this snippet of news, and my fists automatically curl by my sides as anger seeps into my blood sending it pumping around my body. What kind of man talks a girl into giving away her virginity like that, knowing she wanted to wait? Piper notices my mood change and shakes her head. "It wasn't like that. I mean, he didn't force me or anything. I wanted to sleep with him . . . I think."

"You think?" I repeat.

"I was sixteen. Does any girl of that age really know what they want? All I knew is I wanted him to love me the way I loved him. I thought by sleeping with him, that would happen."

"But it didn't?"

"He didn't light candles or put rose petals on my bed. He didn't even stay the night." She gives a weak smile. "He's never actually stayed the night."

"He's an arse, Piper. You deserve so much more."

ANTON

"The heart wants what it wants. According to Emily Dickinson, anyway."

I stand. "Fuck Emily Dickinson, and fuck Hulk. What do they know?"

"She knew quite a lot, actually, being a famous poet and all." Piper grins.

I reach into the wardrobe, pull out a fresh white shirt, and throw it to the bed. "You can take the bed. I'll take the couch."

"You live here?"

"I stay often."

She smirks. "I can go home. It's not late."

"Stay, get some rest. I imagine you need it after days of worrying about Mae." I begin to unfasten my shirt. "You take the bathroom first. Your face is a mess, all that crying and shit," I say playfully, and she laughs again.

"You're a secret gentleman."

"Don't tell anyone. All the girls will want a piece."

Piper looks back at me from the bathroom doorway. "If we're sticking to the plan, you're off the market." Then she disappears inside.

I stare at the closed door. The plan seemed like a good idea, but the more time I spend with

Piper, the more I want to turn my plan into a reality. The thought unsettles me.

I don't sleep a wink. The sound of Piper's light breathing keeps me awake. I picture holding her while she sleeps, and I try to imagine how she would feel lying naked in my arms.

My mobile buzzes to life and I snatch it up before it wakes Piper. It's Michael, so I step out of the room onto the balcony. "Yeah?"

"I've got his right-hand man." His voice is gruff.

"Lorenzo's?" I ask. "How? Where?" We've been looking at Lorenzo's close circle for months. Alexander disappeared as soon as Lorenzo did, and you can bet your life he knows exactly where Lorenzo is hiding out.

"Would you believe the fucker walked into a strip club in Essex?"

"Essex?" I repeat. "What the fuck are you doing in Essex? And where is he now?"

"I like Essex. He's in the boot of my car."

ANTON

I take a minute to get my head straight. "You're one weird motherfucker." I sigh. "Okay, take him to the house. I'll meet you there."

I disconnect the call and dial Hulk's number. I could take it directly to Ace, but after everything he's been through, I'm sure he needs a good night's sleep, and I want an excuse to piss off Hulk. "What the fuck are you calling me for?" he snaps as soon as he answers. "It's four in the morning."

"Do you think I'd be calling you if it wasn't important? I'd much rather be in my bed with your beautiful lady."

"You're with Piper?" he growls, and I smile to myself. I want him to suffer.

"I bet you're regretting passing her up right now, big man."

"Fuck you, Anton, you piece of shit. I'll get her back if it's the last thing I ever do. She loves me, you prick. All I have to do is click my fingers and she'll be on her knees." He's riled, and it satisfies me.

"But now I've taken her, she belongs to me. If you take her, I'll have to kill you, and we both know you don't value Piper enough to risk your life."

"She'll never be with you, Anton. She loves me."

"Not what she was saying just an hour ago, my friend. When Ace is up to it, tell him I have one of the packages we've been searching for. It's not the main one, but it may lead us there." I disconnect the call.

"You have someone connected to Lorenzo?" Piper gasps from behind me.

"You shouldn't be listening in to people's calls," I say, turning to face her. Standing barefoot in my shirt, she is a sight to behold, and I crave her skin against my own.

"If you don't want me to hear private calls, then you shouldn't answer the phone."

"I thought you were sleeping."

"I was, but I had a dream and . . ." She stops and blushes, giving away that the dream involved me. "Never mind."

I move towards her, and she backs up until she's standing at the foot of the bed. "You need to get some sleep. I'll send a driver to collect you in a few hours." I pull back the sheets, and she climbs back into bed.

I dress quickly. "Anton, how will the plan work between us?"

ANTON

"What do you mean?" I ask.

"How do we deal with . . . needs?"

I smirk. "Take a cold shower. It works wonders." I pick up my car keys and mobile and lean over the bed where she lays to place a kiss on her head. "Rest. Call me when you wake and I'll have a car get you. Please do not leave this hotel alone." I head for the door. "Oh, and was I just good or was I amazing?" She figures that I'm referring to her dream, so she blushes again and throws a pillow in my direction. Her laughter rings out as I leave with a smile on my face.

Chapter Seven

ANTON

I'm waiting outside when Michael arrives. He stops the car inside the garage and pops open the boot. I look down at Alexander's huddled form. His putrid smell fills my nostrils. He smells like he's pissed himself and drank half a gallon of whiskey. His glazed eyes reach mine, and he smirks. Michael tugs the rag tied around his mouth down a little. "Alexander, you've been a hard man to find," I say.

He grins. "I took a piss in your lovely car."

"Still as charming as ever." I sigh. "Get him in the basement." I step out the garage and take in a lungful of fresh air. The garage covers a secret tunnel that my father had built. It goes under the house and leads to several rooms.

ANTON

These rooms have seen some brutal killings, especially under my father's reign.

My mind wanders back to Piper, and I find myself smiling. "What got you all happy?" Ella joins me in the garden, hugging a cup of coffee.

"Why are awake so early?" I ask. Of course, I already know the answer is because she's plagued by nightmares. She sees a therapist every week, but it doesn't seem to be helping.

"Mum had a bad night," she says. I grit my teeth in agitation, and Ella spots it. "She can't help it, Anton. She's depressed."

"About what?" I snap. I'm tired of her self-pity.

"You know what about. She loved Dad and she misses him. Despite what he did."

"Despite what he did," I repeat, rolling my eyes, "he doesn't deserve her love, or anyone's for that matter. She needs to stop now. I'm losing patience with her, Ella."

"She can't just stop being depressed. It's an illness. With our support, she'll come out of it in her own time."

I shake my head, doubting that very much. "I'll talk to her later."

"Maybe that's not such a good idea when you're so mad at her. I could do without you upsetting her and sending her back instead of forward."

"I'm going to talk to her," I say firmly. "As the head of this household, I'm laying down some new rules." I turn to go inside the house, but Ella takes my arm to stop me.

"Please, Anton. Let me deal with her. I can feel a breakthrough coming at any time." I pull my arm free and go inside. This has to be done.

I work out for an hour in the gym attached to my office. I have too much energy right now. Usually, I'd burn that off with women, but lately, I can only think of one woman I want, and she's not an option at the moment.

I shower and then spend some time in the office before Michael enters. "I picked up Piper and drove her home."

"Thank you. I appreciate it. Was she okay?"

ANTON

"Smiling from ear to ear. What did you do to make her smile like that?" He smirks and takes a seat.

"Not what you're thinking."

"No?" He looks surprised.

"The plan has changed slightly." Michael sits forward with interest. "I'm going to marry her for real."

He laughs, throwing his head back until he almost chokes. "Sorry, what?"

"She can handle shit. She makes me laugh. She's hot. She knows how to behave at dinner parties. What's not to like?"

"I thought you were doing this to piss off Hulk and appease the capos. Now, you're telling me this is real?"

I shrug my shoulders and rub at the stubble on my chin. "I don't know. There's something about her, Michael."

"And she's happy with this new plan, is she?" he asks sceptically.

"She doesn't know. I need to take baby steps with her."

"Baby steps?" Michael laughs again. "Are you shitting me? You've taken her on two dates, and now, you're saying that you're marrying her and she doesn't even know. Are we also forgetting the fact she's in love with someone else?"

I grin. "Minor details."

Michael stands, still shaking his head in disbelief. "I hate to think of the body count when this all goes wrong and you go off on a rampage."

"It won't go wrong. Have a little faith in your boss."

"Oh, I have faith, but I've seen love, and if she truly loves him, you've got no chance."

He leaves, and I pick up my phone. Maybe he's right, but going on the past between her and Hulk, I'll have no trouble winning her over. I've just got to make her see I'm the better option. I fire off a quick text to her to let her know I'm thinking about her.

PIPER

I lean back on my hands and allow the sunshine to warm my face. Mae is struggling today, and Ace won't let her have any visitors. A shadow falls over me and I open one eye to see Hulk staring down at me. "S'up?" he grumbles.

"Not much. You okay?"

ANTON

He lowers himself to sit next to me. "Relieved to have the Pres back." He stares straight ahead before adding, "I spoke to your boyfriend early this morning." I remain quiet. I hate lying, and I don't want to agree that Anton is my boyfriend because that's a lie. "You sleep with him yet, Piper?"

I feel my face slowly turning crimson with embarrassment. "That's none of your business, Hulk."

"It is when you still sleep with me."

I gasp. "I haven't slept with you in weeks."

"There was a time when you were seeing him in the beginning that you'd slept with me."

He's referring to the time I went to Tag for help and he passed it to Anton, who dropped something to help me. At the time, Hulk was being a prick, treating it like a pissing contest, and Mum came to my rescue, making it very clear I was free to see whomever I wanted. Hulk just assumed the worst, and I didn't bother to correct him. I lower my eyes to the dirt. "Hulk, you and I aren't together. Whatever I do with Anton, or anyone else for that matter, is none of your business. You sleep with other people all the time and I just have to suck it up. This is what you wanted, right, to be free and single?"

"Maybe I can take you out," he blurts out, and I stare at him wide-eyed, waiting for his next words. "I mean, I know I can't do fancy shit like dinners with the mayor, but I know a mean curry house, and I know how much you love a good curry."

I smile because he remembers the small details, even though he hates to admit it. "You want to take me out? Like on a date or something?"

Hulk shifts uncomfortably and begins to rake his fingers in the dirt. "Yeah, I guess it could be a date." My heart beats wildly. He's never uttered the word 'date' to me since the day he realised how much I liked him.

"Okay," I say, nodding, and he side-eyes me. "I'm serious," I confirm. "If you want to take me out, I'd like that."

He grins. "Okay, it's a date. I'll book us a table for tonight." He jumps up and rushes inside.

My mobile alerts me to a message and I pull it from my pocket. It's a text from Anton.

Anton: Tell me more about your dream. What were we doing?

ANTON

I smile wider, enjoying this new playful side to him.

Me: I didn't say you were part of my dream. Guess who asked me on a date just now. Hulk!! The plan is working. He wants to take me to my favourite food place.

A small part of me wonders if this will bother Anton, but it was his idea after all. He told me Hulk would come running the second he thought I was serious about someone else. I wait for the reply, but it doesn't immediately come. The longer I wait, the more worried I become, so I send another.

Me: Are you mad at me? I thought this was the whole point.

A minute later, it pings, and I feel relief as I open the message.

Anton: In a meeting. Talk later.

Something feels off with his short answer. His playful side has gone, and I have a heaviness in my heart like I've done something wrong.

It gets to eight in the evening, and I dress for my date with Hulk. I'm still feeling weird and can't shake the feeling that this is wrong.

Usually, Mae would be here helping me, but she's been so tired since she returned, and I didn't want to bother her. I throw my hair up then take it back down because it reminds me too much of my date with Anton. I change into jeans but then hate the way they cling to my arse, so I swap them for a short summer dress.

By the time I get downstairs, Hulk is pacing. He's wearing his usual jeans and T-shirt along with his club kutte. "We'll be late if you don't get a move on," he huffs, and my heart squeezes. Earlier, he was sweet and bashful, now he's back to snapping and being irritable.

My mum smiles from the couch, where she's sitting curled up next to my dad. "You look pretty, baby girl," she says. At least someone noticed.

I follow Hulk outside. He throws his leg over his bike and stares at me expectantly. I look down at my short dress. It's the kind that has a flowing skirt, and the second he moves the bike, it'll be blowing up around my neck. "I'm not really dressed for the bike, Hulk," I point out.

ANTON

"I'm a biker. I travel by bike."

"But I dressed for a date, not a ride on your bike. Can't we take a car?" I ask through gritted teeth. Hulk sighs and gets off the bike, then he goes to the gatehouse and swaps the keys for a club car.

By the time we make it to the restaurant, we're ten minutes late and Hulk is stressed. He stomps inside, and I practically run behind to catch up with his long strides. It's hardly a great start to our first date.

The waiter pulls out my chair as I sit opposite Hulk. "What can I get you to drink?" the waiter asks politely.

"I'll take a bourbon," Hulk grumbles, picking up the menu and opening it. When he makes no move to order my drink, I smile weakly at the waiter and add a glass of white wine to the order. I know I shouldn't compare this date to the ones I had with Anton, but somehow, I keep doing it, and it's making me feel disappointed.

Glancing around at the candle-lit tables, other couples are all chatting animatedly. I close my eyes for a brief moment and take a breath, warning myself to stop comparing. Hulk is different, and that's one of the reasons I like him.

"This is nice, isn't it?" I ask brightly.

Hulk continues to stare at his menu. "If you like sitting with strangers less than two feet away and eating overpriced food."

"Why did you choose this place if it's overpriced?"

"Because it had a free table. The others I tried were fully booked."

I change the subject. "It makes a nice change to get out of the club together. We've never done this before."

Hulk hands me the menu. "I suppose."

The waiter returns with our drinks "So, are you and Anton together?" he asks.

"We've been on two dates. What about you?" I ask. "Are you seeing anyone?"

"You know I don't have relationships, Piper."

"You used to tell me you don't date, yet here we are."

ANTON

He ignores my comment and looks around uncomfortably. "I didn't know you liked this kind of thing."

"All women like to be treated once in a while, Hulk," I say with a little laugh.

I stare at him for a few moments. He's gorgeous but in a different way to Anton. They're both well-built men, but where Hulk has a roughness about him, Anton has an air of importance. They both appear confident and strong. While Hulk prefers his jeans and T-shirts, Anton dresses in tailor-made suits. I drain my glass and sigh. *Why am I comparing them when Hulk is the man I love?*

"I've never had to do any of this for a woman before," he says.

"You don't have to do it now, Hulk. You asked me on a date. I haven't forced you into it."

Hulk sighs. "I have competition now though. He flashed the cash and off you ran."

I'm insulted that he's insinuating I'm only interested in Anton for his money. It's not like Hulk doesn't have any. All the guys at the club live a comfortable life. "You think I'm that shallow?"

"I don't know, Piper. I feel like I don't know you very well at all lately. Lucy said the same. She's worried about you."

"You talked to Lucy about me?" I know they share the same dad, but still, it feels weird knowing they've discussed me.

"You're acting differently. It feels like you're trying to be something you're not to impress Anton."

I'm so angry, I could burst. "In what way?" I ask as calmly as I can. I know I haven't changed. This is all bullshit. "I think you're both just pissed because you don't like Anton, and you don't like the thought of me being with him. Maybe the change you're both seeing is happiness?"

"He's an arrogant prick. I don't like him, and I don't think he's good enough for you. He lied to Lucy and told her Tag was dead. She grieved for him—"

"That was to protect Tag," I cut in.

"It's not the point. His number one priority is the organisation. It always will be."

"And yours is The Rebellion," I snap. "You're no different."

"The last time I checked, you were a part of The Rebellion."

The waiter returns to take our order, and it's the temporary break we need to collect our thoughts. We both order a chicken curry and hand our menus back. Once he's gone, I take a deep, calming breath. "Why did you ask me on this date, Hulk?"

He fiddles with his knife for a moment before looking directly into my eyes. "I like you, Piper. We've spent so many years either fighting or fucking, but we've never labelled it. I feel like I'm being backed into a corner and have to make us official before you're snatched away from me."

I frown in confusion. It doesn't sound like a declaration of love. "What are you saying?"

"That maybe it's time to label us. To stop fucking about and try to be together."

I let his words sink in. "If Anton wasn't on the scene right now, would you be saying any of this?" I brace myself because I know his answer may slay me.

"Probably not right now. But like Scar said to me, sometimes it takes someone else coming along to make you see what you want, and I think I want you. I haven't even looked at another woman in weeks. I miss us too much." It's not how I imagined our relationship starting. I mean, I didn't expect hearts and flowers—Hulk's a biker after all—but I don't want him to feel forced into a choice. He stands. "I need to take a piss." I watch his retreating form and then my eyes fall to his mobile phone sitting on the table. I bite on my lower lip. I shouldn't look, but something inside is telling me to, so I pick it up.

I enter his passcode, which has always been his date of birth. Predictably, it opens, and I go straight to his calls, but there's nothing that stands out. Next, I open his messages. I'm not shocked to see girls' names. Most of his texts are to and from females. I open the last message he sent, and it's to a girl named Tanya. I don't recognise the name. The message to her was sent five minutes before our date began.

Tanya: Hey gorgeous, what are you up to? I'm lonely.

Hulk: Not a lot, baby girl. Want me to come over later?

Tanya: Sure.

Hulk: I've got a meeting but should be done in an hour or so, that work for you?
Tanya: I'll be ready and waiting . . .

I flick through their other messages to each other. It sounds like he's been sleeping with her for some weeks. So much for not looking at anyone else because he misses us.

I'm about to set the mobile back on the table when a message from Lucy flashes up.

Lucy: Have you had any luck talking sense into her yet?

My hands shake as I replace it back on his side of the table. I feel like I've been ambushed and this whole date was his way of getting me alone to lecture me about Anton.

When he returns, the waiter is just arriving with our food. We wait patiently while he sets it down, and once he's gone, Hulk picks up his fork and takes a scoop of the curry. He nods in approval. "I'll drop you home when we're done. I hope you don't mind, but I've got some business to attend to and I don't want you to think this date is a way for me to get into your bed. I'm trying to do this shit properly," he lies.

"Is 'business' code word for Tanya?" I ask, arching a brow.

Hulk pauses, his fork halfway to his mouth. His eyes fall to his mobile. "You went through my phone?"

"I'm not proud, but it's the person you've turned me into." I bury my face in my hands. "I just can't trust you, so I find myself sneaking around and checking your messages. This date bullshit was an excuse, wasn't it? You knew I'd jump at the chance, so you dangled the carrot, and all along it was a way to get me alone so you could talk shit about me and Anton and try to put me off. I expected it from you, but Lucy?"

"Like I said, we're worried."

"Worried or jealous?" I snap. "If I was seeing anyone other than Anton, I don't think you'd give a shit, but you know he's a real threat."

"I know he's in the fucking mob, Piper. He's no good for you."

I scoff. "He's given me no reason to think that. He treats me well, he looks after me, and he doesn't complain about doing simple things like having dinner together. I'm not an inconvenience to him and I'm not second best."

"We're meant to be, Piper, you know we are," Hulk argues.

I shake my head. "You're not ready, and I'm not waiting around. You and Lucy need to stop meddling because all you're doing is pushing me closer to him." I throw my napkin down and stand. "I hate to break it to you, Hulk, but I deserve better than what you're offering."

ANTON

Since my father died, my mother stays in her bedroom, where she keeps the curtains closed, shutting out any light at all. *No wonder she's depressed.* I stand in the open doorway, yet I still feel suffocated by this darkness. She doesn't move from the chair in the corner. Instead, she sits staring at the floor. Her nightdress is the blue silk one that my father brought her from Italy on his very last trip.

I march over to the curtains and pull them back, allowing the moonlight to stream in. I push open a window and breathe in the fresh night air.

Keeping my back to her, in a low tone, I say, "It's time to stop this now, Mother." Of course, she doesn't respond, but I know she hears me. "I've sent countless psychotherapists in here to assess you. I've spent money on therapists in case you needed to talk. They all tell me you'll come around in your own time. That this is some kind of grieving process." I turn to face her. "And yet still, you stare at the damn carpet like you expect my father to miraculously fucking reappear from hell!" I shout the last few words, and her body jerks in fright. "So, I'm in here to tell you that it's time to stop now." I wait a few beats, but she doesn't move. "Right." I sigh. "Fine. I'm having you committed to a private hospital where they can manage you."

I walk towards the door, and she suddenly jumps up and takes my arm. I stare down at her bony fingers as they grip my jacket. "No. Please." The words come out as a whisper.

"This behaviour isn't fair on Ella," I snap, shaking her off me. "Pull yourself out of whatever hole you're in and be a mother again."

A tear slips down her pale cheek. "I miss him, Anton. I know I shouldn't, but I miss him so much." The last few words come out high-pitched as tears fill her eyes.

"You can't miss a man who was so evil. Forget about him."

"You blame me." She sniffles. "I see it in your eyes."

ANTON

"It doesn't matter what I think. We have to help Ella through this. As her mother, that's your job."

"I didn't know. I swear, I didn't."

I get close to her, shoving my face in hers. "And if you had known, would you have stopped it? You never stood up to him. You were too scared."

Ella appears in the doorway. Her smile fades as she senses the mood in the room. "What's going on?" she asks. She takes Mum by the arm and leads her back to her chair like she's some delicate flower ready to break.

"She's going to a private hospital. I'll make the arrangements." I storm out the room and head for my office. Ella is hot on my tail. She slams the door closed and glares at me.

"No." She says it like she believes she has any input in this. I laugh at her attempt to stand up to me. "I'm looking after her. She doesn't need a hospital."

"It's not your decision. I want her gone so that you can heal."

"I *am* healed," she growls angrily, almost stamping her foot. "Why are you waiting for me to fall apart? She is allowed to miss her husband."

"No, she isn't. He was a monster. He doesn't deserve to be missed."

Ella screams angrily, balling her fists by her side, and it reminds me of when she was a little girl, throwing a tantrum to get her own way. "If you send her away, I'll never speak to you again," she warns.

"You will. I hold your credit cards. Get out, I have work to do."

She goes towards the door but pauses with her hand on the knob. "You know that sending her away won't make the guilt go away, Anton." She pauses for a beat, then adds, "You didn't know. I don't blame you or Mum for any of it." Then she leaves, and I stare at the closed door, ignoring the ache in my chest.

I pick up my mobile. There's a message from Piper.

Piper: Sorry.

I check the time. It's just after nine, so she must still be on her date with Hulk. My mind runs into overtime. Is she sorry because she's slept with him? Is it because she's backing out of the plan?

ANTON

Letting her go on this stupid date was tough, but I fully expected him to fuck it up and she needed to see that. I throw my phone in my top drawer and slam it closed, hoping I wasn't wrong and it hasn't cost me her.

Chapter Eight

PIPER

It's been a few days since my disastrous date with Hulk. We aren't speaking, which is not unusual for us. Fighting is what we do best. And I haven't heard from Anton. Despite wanting to send a string of texts, I haven't because he didn't respond when I apologised for going on the date with Hulk, which tells me I've blown it.

The men have gone out on business, which leaves me to watch over Mae. She's doing so much better, but Ace still insists that she isn't ready to leave her room.

She buries her nose into Dodge's fur. "What do you think about me and Hulk, Mae?"

ANTON

Without looking up, she laughs. "I'm so confused. You and Hulk, then you and Anton, and now, you're back to Hulk. What's going on?"

"I just want your opinion. We've spent years talking about marrying bikers and becoming ol' ladies. Do you think I'll marry Hulk one day?"

"I've never really imagined you with anyone else, but that's because you've only ever talked about Hulk. There's never been anyone else for you."

The door opens and Ace steps inside. Dodge jumps from the bed, excited to see his owner. Ace kisses Mae on the head and strokes her face. "Are you okay?" She nods, then Ace turns to me and hands me a black box. "This is for you." It's wrapped in a red ribbon and there's a label which reads, 'To help with things when you're dreaming of me'.

I smile and my heart rate picks up. "Anton gave you this?"

"Yep. Apparently, I'm a delivery man these days," says Ace dryly.

I give Mae a kiss on the cheek before leaving them together. I want to open this in the privacy of my own room.

I sit in the centre of my bed and cross my legs. I place the box in front of me, carefully pull the ribbon, and lift the lid. Inside the box, there's bright pink tissue paper. I rummage through to find another box. Pulling it out, I laugh out loud. In my hand is a vibrator. I send him a text.

Me: *Thank you. This will help a lot.*

I get into bed with a smile on my face, which makes a nice change. I feel my eyes grow heavy and I'm drifting off with thoughts of Anton filling my head.

When I open my eyes, it's dark outside. I realise my mobile is buzzing along the bedside table, so I reach for it, rubbing my eyes and yawning. It's Anton. I answer it, noticing the time is three in the morning. "I have to see you, Piper." His voice is low, almost a growl.

"Right now?" I ask. "It's the early hours of the morning."

"It's nothing to do with the plan. I need a friendly face." He pauses. "I need you." He sounds vulnerable. It's something I never expected to hear from Anton, and I place my mobile between my shoulder and my ear as I climb from my bed and pull a hoodie from my wardrobe. "Can I come by now and get you?" he asks.

"Yes." I don't hesitate in my answer because something about his tone calls to me.

"I'll be outside in two minutes," he says, and then the line goes dead. I pull on the hoodie, which hangs over the shorts I wore to bed, and slip my feet into my trainers. I pull my hair into a messy bun as I sneak downstairs.

The night air is cold as I rush outside and make my way to the gate just as Anton's car slows to a stop.

Michael gets out the driver's side and smiles. "Morning," he says. "He's a bit of a mess, Piper. Be prepared." He opens the back door, and I slide into the warmth of the car. Anton is slumped in the seat. His white shirt is stained crimson with blood and his head is resting back.

"Jesus," I hiss, kneeling beside him and opening his jacket. "Are you hurt?" I ask, running my hands over his chest to feel for a wound.

He takes me by the wrists and stills me. "It's not my blood."

"Oh," I breathe, "good."

Anton sniggers. "You're relieved that someone else is hurt?"

"No. I'm relieved it isn't you." And I realise I mean those words.

He stares at me for a long time before wrapping an arm around my waist and pulling me to sit over his lap. I snake my arms around his shoulders and lay my head against him. We stay like that until we arrive at his home.

Michael opens the car door, and Anton slides out with me in his arms. He lowers me down his body until my feet hit the ground and then he takes me by the hand. The lights are on, and he exchanges a wary look with Michael.

The front door swings open, making me flinch. Ella stands before us, her face red with anger. "I fucking hate you!" she screams towards Anton. Michael places himself in front of me as Anton releases my hand. "How could you do this when I begged you not to?"

"I told you my reasons. I will not discuss it any more." Anton's tone is blunt and cold.

"Fuck you and fuck your reasons. She tried to overdose tonight." Ella's sentence hangs in the air for a moment. "You would know that if you ever answered your fucking phone," she screams, and then she strikes Anton across the face. I hold my breath, waiting for his reaction, but Michael rushes forward, scooping Ella up and taking her inside.

A second later, as we step into the house, Hulk appears from the living room looking sheepish. "What are you doing here?" growls Anton. His tone is deadly, and I shudder.

Michael places Ella on her feet but remains in front of her, keeping her a good distance from Anton. "I invited him," she spits angrily. "When I couldn't get a hold of you, I tried the clubhouse. I needed support."

Anton's deadly stare fixes on his sister. "You called the club and asked a biker to come and support you?"

"I'm offended," says Hulk, squaring his shoulders like he's readying for a fight. "She got upset on the phone. I was trying to do a nice thing."

I raise my eyebrow sceptically. "And you just love to rescue a damsel," I mutter.

"You know me, Piper, always happy to lend a hand." I roll my eyes. "Actually, can we have a chat . . . outside?"

"No," snaps Anton, grabbing my hand again.

I give it a reassuring squeeze. "You need a minute to speak to Ella," I say calmly. "I'll be fine." He holds my stare for a few seconds before eventually releasing me.

Outside, Hulk turns on me as soon as the door is closed. "Why in the hell are you here in your pyjamas in the middle of the night? Did you sneak out of the clubhouse?"

"I didn't break any rules, Hulk. I'm single and old enough to make my own choices. I would have texted my mum in the morning."

"It's freezing and you're here in your bed shorts," he snaps. "You're clearly a booty call."

"You're just pissed because I'm not your booty call anymore. Why did you come to Ella's rescue? She's delicate, Hulk. Please don't use her to get back at Anton."

Hulk laughs sarcastically. "Please," he mutters. "Do you really think you're worth that? I've moved on from you."

I squash down the hurt. "You never really started with me. I didn't come out here so you could make me feel like shit again. Ella's a nice girl. She deserves a nice guy."

He takes a deep breath and rubs at his forehead. "I spend days thinking of things to say to

ANTON

you just so I can hear your voice." He laughs to himself, turning away from me. "I hate it when you're mad at me, which is most of the time. And when I finally get the chance to talk to you, everything comes out wrong and I say shit I don't mean. I'm sorry I always upset you, Piper."

I'm taken aback by his honesty and my heart melts a little. "I guess we both say the wrong thing."

"I hate that you're here with him," he almost whispers, turning back to face me. He steps closer and laces his fingers with mine. "It's killing me, Pip." His lips are on mine before I have a chance to register that he's moved so close. His hands release mine and move up, cupping my jaw. Our tongues begin a slow dance until I hear the door open. It breaks the spell, and I step back, wiping my mouth on the back of my hand. I stare at Hulk wide-eyed.

"Sorry to spoil the moment, Piper, but get inside." Anton sounds calm, but when I look at his face, I see the storm in his eyes.

"She doesn't have to go with you if she doesn't want to. Piper, you can come home with me," Hulk snaps.

I stand between the pair, looking from one to the other. I suddenly feel like one of those puppies you sometimes see on the internet, where their owners place themselves either side and shout the puppy's name until he chooses who he loves more.

ANTON

I wait patiently for Piper to come to me, but when it's clear she's indecisive, I pull out my ace card. "Actually, she does have to come inside. We have a recording to view. Don't we, Piper? Remember . . . from the club?" Her face falls when she realises it's a veiled threat, then she pushes past me and comes inside. I smile at Hulk and then give him a small wave before slamming the door in his face. The urge to have him killed weighs heavy on my mind. I don't want him near Piper or Ella.

It's quiet inside. Ella has taken herself off to bed in a mood, and Michael is in the office, putting a call in to check on my mother. I find Piper pacing in the living room. "What the hell was that?" she spits angrily.

"A reminder of the reason we're doing this."

"But I thought . . ." She pauses. "Never mind."

ANTON

"I still need you for my plan. You might have gotten what you want with Hulk, but you're helping me."

"I thought you were upset. That's why I agreed to come. I thought you needed me."

I don't tell her that she's correct and that the reason I called was I'd just had my hands over two stab wounds in one of my capos as he lay dying. I don't tell her that I left the hospital after waiting most of the night for news only to find out he'd died, and the only person I wanted was her. Seeing her with Hulk, their tongues down each other's throat, woke me up. It was the ice bucket I needed to remind me that Piper is serving a purpose. Now, more than ever, I need my men to see me as their leader.

"We're going to Italy," I announce. "Michael is going to book our flights shortly. It'll be for a few days."

"I can't just go to Italy," she scoffs.

"I'm not asking. Get some sleep." I turn my back to her, dismissing her.

"Who the fuck are you talking to?" she suddenly snaps. "How dare you order me like that and then turn your back? I'm not your personal whore."

I spin fast, taking her by surprise. Backing her up to the wall, I push my face close to hers. I see her fear, but she tries her hardest not to let it show. "Tonight, I lost a good man. I come home to find my mother has attempted suicide and my sister is alone with a fucking biker. I am not about to fight with you on this. Until I'm done with you, you will behave exactly like my whore and do as you are fucking told or I will send that tape to your father. Then I'll tell Hulk how you aborted his baby in some backstreet clinic, paid for by the mob." It's a low blow, but I've been pushed to the edge tonight, and I can't control myself any longer.

Piper's eyes fill with tears. I expect a slap or an object to come flying towards me, but she doesn't move a muscle. We haven't spoken about the clinic that I'd sorted out for her. Months ago, Piper had asked Lucy and Tag to help her, but they were newlyweds and going on their honeymoon, so Tag passed it to me. I know the clinic well, and they were happy to help me out. Two thousand cash and Piper's problem went away.

I step back from her. "Get some sleep, Piper. We'll be leaving at some point tomorrow."

ANTON

Instead, she hooks her fingers into the waistband of her shorts and pushes them down her legs. I stare at her, dumbfounded. She isn't wearing underwear. Her shaven pussy is right in front of me, and it takes all my control not to drop to my knees just to taste her once. "What are you doing?" I croak, my throat suddenly dry.

"Well, if I'm your whore, then get it over and done with." She pulls her hoodie over her head, leaving her in just a strappy pyjama top. When she takes that in her hands, I rush forward and grab her wrists to stop her from removing that too.

"Stop," I growl. "You've made your point. I didn't mean whore. You said that word first. I'm not going to have sex with you, so put your clothes back on." When I'm sure she won't remove any more clothes, I release her wrists.

She pulls her shorts up. "Thank you," she says, jutting out her chin.

"For what?"

"Reminding me what arseholes men are. For a second, I forgot we were playing a game, acting as part of a plan. I almost thought we were friends." Her eyes are sad, and I bite my inner cheek to stop me from making a fool of myself by telling her how I really feel about her.

"You needed reminding. I have a plan, and you can't fuck it up because of your silly little high school crush on Hulk. Goodnight." I watch as she stomps from the room and heads up the stairs. I take the stairs two at a time, and when I reach the top, I begin to unfasten my blood-soaked shirt. She stops when she realises she has no idea where she's going and folds her arms over her chest stubbornly. I hide my smirk. She's still sassy even when she's lost. "In here," I say, opening the bedroom door across from my own. She pushes past me like a sulky teenager, but I catch her eyes assessing my tattooed chest.

I remain in the doorway, staring down at the shirt that's now in my hands. I see Luke's face flash before my eyes. Even the biggest men have a look of fear in their eyes when they see the end coming.

"Were you close?" asks Piper. I shake my head to snap me from my daydream, and Piper is in front of me with concern in her eyes. "You said one of your men died." She takes another step closer and reaches her hand out to take my own. The image of her kissing Hulk flashes in front of me and I back out of the room before she can bewitch me with her touch.

"Goodnight, Piper."

I head back down to the office. The sun will be rising soon, but I'm too pumped to get any sleep. Michael is staring at the wall with an empty glass in his hand. "Rough night," I mutter, and he snaps from his thoughts.

"You ever gotten sick of the nightclubs?" he asks. I take a seat behind my desk and signal for him to continue. "There're too many chancers out there these days. It isn't like it was before when your dad first opened the clubs. That guy tonight wasn't even from London. He's a nobody and he took out Luke just like that."

"He's a dead nobody now." I sigh, but Michael's right, the clubs are dangerous. They're attracting the wrong kind of people, and the kids who drink in there aren't scared of anyone or anything. They'll die for no cause at all just because someone knocked into them by mistake. Luke had stepped into someone else's argument tonight. He was trying to calm the situation to stop the police from turning up, and he ended up getting stabbed by a no-mark piece of shit. "It's all part of this world, isn't it?"

"No," says Michael coldly. "Not anymore. There're no rules. No respect."

"Get some sleep," I suggest. "It's been a rough night. Did you sort the flights for Italy?"

Michael nods. "Private plane. Noon. They're expecting us. His mother was beside herself."

"She's lost her only son, and he didn't leave an heir."

"Makes ya think, doesn't it? I thought your plan with Piper was crazy, but then something like this happens and you see how quickly your family name is gone. Suddenly, I don't think your plan is crazy anymore," says Michael thoughtfully. "If I were you and I had that fine piece of arse right upstairs, I wouldn't be here talking to you." He leaves, slapping me on the shoulder.

※

I wake at my desk. The sunlight beams in, and I blink in protest then move my neck from side to side. I really have to stop falling asleep in this

ANTON

office. It's almost ten in the morning, and we have a plane to catch. I open the office door and hear laughter coming from the kitchen. It's a nice sound, and I gravitate towards it.

Penny, our housekeeper, is humming to herself while frying eggs. Piper and Ella are watching something on a mobile phone, laughing uncontrollably, and Michael is watching the pair fondly.

I stand in the doorway and take in the sight. It's been a while since this place heard laughter, and it warms my heart. Both women must sense me standing here around the same time and they look up. Their smiles fade and they both lower back into their seats. Penny brings their plates to the table full of bacon and eggs. "Good morning, Mr. Martinez," Penny says, bowing her head slightly. I return her smile and take my usual seat at the head of the table.

Michael picks up his newspaper and begins to scan it. The girls remain silent, and I'm reminded of when my father was alive. He could kill the happiness in the room too, just by entering it.

Penny slides plates in front of me and Michael. I haven't showered from last night, and the last thing I feel like doing is eating. "We fly at noon. I'll take you home to pack some clothes, Piper," I say.

"I'll drive her," Ella suggests.

I shake my head, knowing her game. "I've told you already. You are not to see that biker again."

"I don't want to. He was just helping me out."

"Anyway, he's not interested in you. He was kissing Piper on the doorstep," I say, and everyone's eyes turn to Piper. She blushes as I leave my untouched breakfast on the table. "I need to shower. Be ready in ten, Piper, and we'll go get your stuff."

Chapter Nine

PIPER

I check through my bag one last time. My mum reaches her hand inside and fishes out a bright pink thong. I snatch it back and stuff it deeper into the bag. "Why Italy?" she asks.

"Why not? I think Anton has business there."

"Are you with him? As in a relationship?"

I shrug and zip the bag up. "We haven't really discussed it. Would it upset you if we were?"

"Nope," she says, popping the P. "Not as long as you're happy. And, secretly, I'm happy you're not dating a biker, but don't tell your dad that."

I laugh. "You don't like bikers?"

"I just want more for my baby girl." She stands and tucks my hair behind my ear. "I love your pops, but not once has he ever taken me outta this country. The club comes first, and I don't begrudge that. I love The Rebellion. But if you have the chance to see the world, then take it."

"Relax, Mum. It's a few days in Italy, not an around-the-world trip. Keep an eye on Mae for me and call me if anything happens with her." I kiss her on the cheek and grab my bag. "And don't tell Pops until I've gone. I don't need that kind of stress."

We get to the airport, and Michael drives us straight onto the tarmac. "Don't we have to go into the airport first?" I ask, stepping out onto the runway.

"Not today." Anton hands my bag to a man in a steward's uniform and then takes my hand and pulls me towards a small plane. We climb the steps and are met at the door by a pretty stewardess. She greets us warmly and shows us into the plane, where Michael is already taking his seat along with a few other men. I spot Ella at the back of the plane, and while Anton shakes hands with the others, I take my seat by her.

ANTON

After last night, I don't want to spend the next few hours with Anton.

Once we're in the air, Ella asks the stewardess for a bottle of cava. Every so often, I feel Anton's eyes glance in our direction. I feel like he's disapproving, but he's in deep conversation with a few of the men and it doesn't look like he'll be getting away anytime soon, so I let Ella fill my glass and relax. "So, you and Hulk, huh?" Ella asks.

"It's not like that. We aren't together. The kiss just happened. Sometimes it's like that with Hulk, but he isn't relationship material. I've spent a long time praying that he'd change, but I'm finally starting to see that he won't." The confession takes me by surprise. *Am I starting to get over Hulk?*

"He has player written all over his sexy backside," Ella says, and I clink my glass with hers. When I first met Ella, I thought she was a cow. Maybe the stories I'd heard from Lucy had swayed my thinking, but I was wrong. The more time I spend with her, the more I like her.

It's a few hours before we land and then another hour of driving before we stop inside the gates of a private villa. I think my jaw hits the floor as I step inside the traditionally decorated house. "We own it," whispers Ella, nudging me towards the stairs. We drank far too much on the flight, and I'm feeling a little giddy as we make our way up. "There's a pool. Get your swimming costume on." She leaves me standing in a bedroom.

There's a large four-poster bed in the centre of the room. It's so big that there's a step going around the bottom to help you climb up. A set of double doors lead onto a balcony. The doors are open, so I step out to take a look at the views. For miles, there are fields, and it's a beautiful sight compared to the dreary London buildings. On the grounds below is a swimming pool surrounded by sun loungers. I rush back into the room and strip off my clothes. I'm just fastening my bikini top when the door opens and Anton waltzes in. He pauses and looks me up and down. "Sorry," I mumble, "Ella said this was my room."

ANTON

"Our room," says Anton as he places his own bag by the bed. "Some of the men who are here with us need to think we're together."

I stare at him, my eyes wide. "What?"

"The plan," he says, looking at me like I'm stupid. "It's part of it."

"You want to pretend to your men that we're a couple? Why do you care if they think we are or not?"

"It's important. You wouldn't understand."

"Try me," I insist. He's making no sense. I thought he was in charge of this organisation.

"The men are losing faith. They want a leader who is settled and gives them hope of an heir to take over after me."

"Wow. That's gone from pretending we're together to providing the Mafia boss with an heir," I screech. "It sounds like a bad romance story."

"Relax," he hisses. "It's a temporary plan to settle them down until I can find a woman worthy of carrying my heir." I raise a surprised brow. I'm not sure if he realises how insulting that last sentence was, and when he eventually looks at my face, he rolls his eyes. "I didn't mean that you aren't worthy."

"What did you mean?" I snap.

"Christ, woman. You don't want to have a baby anyway, so what are you pissed about?"

"Who says I don't want to have a baby?" He stares at me for a moment, and I see that he thinks it's because I chose to have an abortion. "I don't have to justify my decision to you, but the timing wasn't right," I mutter defensively.

"Because of your amazing career?" he asks sarcastically.

"You're being an arse," I snap and snatch my towel from the bed. "For your information, Hulk told me he didn't want kids, and I didn't want to do it alone, so yeah, I chose to abort the baby. It was for the best. No kid wants to grow up with parents who hate each other."

"It didn't look much like hate from where I was standing last night when you kissed him."

I growl in frustration. "He kissed me, and for the first time ever, I felt nothing!" I stomp out the room, kicking myself for blurting out that piece of information.

I find Ella by the pool opening another bottle of something fizzy and alcoholic. I smile when she hands me a glass, and I drink it down in one go. "Thirsty?" she asks.

"Pissed at your brother."

ANTON

"Aren't you guys supposed to be acting as the perfect couple this weekend?"

"That'll be pretty hard when he keeps opening that stupid mouth of his," I grumble. "He doesn't know how to be nice."

"I like you, Piper. I think you're going to be good for Anton," she adds with a wide smile, which makes me smile too.

We spend a couple hours by the pool enjoying the sun's warm rays and chatting about anything and everything.

Anton eventually comes outside and orders that I dress for dinner. I'm dreading the thought of sitting alone with him. His insults are becoming tiresome and draining. Ella asks if she can do my makeup. I feel like she's lacking female company since her mother got sick and she craves it. So, I agree, and she follows me up to get ready.

At nine, I go down to the foyer as instructed and find Anton waiting for me. One thing I've noticed is that he's always punctual.

We take a short walk into a nearby village. It's buzzing with life, and as we pass people sitting idly outside shops and restaurants, they nod in greeting to us.

Anton stops outside a small traditional restaurant. He looks down at me and smiles. "You'll love this place, but I have to warn you that these people are over-the-top crazy and they'll treat you like they've known you for years. I apologise in advance for their overly familiar ways." Before I get a chance to respond, he opens the door and pulls me inside.

It's small—there are maybe six tables and a bar—but it's cosy, and I instantly feel at ease here. There are three old men chatting at the bar, and when they spot Anton, they stand and make lots of noise. They embrace him and kiss him on the back of his hand. One of the men shouts and a female who must be my mum's age appears. She is delighted to see Anton and also embraces him. When they finish fussing around him, he takes my hand and pulls me to stand by his side. He says something in Italian, and they stare wide-eyed at me.

"Finally," the woman says with a smile. She embraces me and kisses my cheeks. "I'm

ANTON

Louisa," she introduces herself. "This is my husband, Franco, and his brothers, Giuseppe and Roberto." They also kiss my cheeks and invite me to sit at their table.

"Louisa makes the best ossobuco. I can highly recommend it," says Anton as Roberto pours us each a glass of red wine. I nod, and Anton asks Louisa for two dishes of ossobuco. I've never heard of it, but I don't mention that because Anton usually chooses the best food.

ANTON

It's relaxing being back in my home country. I don't feel like I have to watch over my shoulder here because everyone respects me. And having Piper here, away from Hulk and Lucy trying to poison her against me, I can really put my plan into action.

I watch as she takes her third shot of limoncello and coughs dramatically. "Your wife drinks like fish," Giuseppe says in Italian, grinning, and I nod. When we arrived, I told them Piper was soon to be my wife. Luckily, she doesn't understand Italian.

Roberto tries to pour her another shot, but I take her hand and pull her to stand. "I think that's enough for tonight."

"I'm fine," Piper protests. "I'm having fun."

"And I don't want to carry you back up the hill," I tease.

We say our goodbyes with a promise to meet them again tomorrow night. Louisa tells me she'll bring the villagers together for a celebration that their capo dei capi is home. I'm not sure Luke's mum will feel much like celebrating when I go to pay my respects tomorrow.

The cool night air is refreshing when we step onto the cobbled street. "I had the best night," breathes Piper, and I smile.

"You're drunk." As if to prove my point, she stumbles, and I have to reach out to catch her. She laughs and throws her arms around me. I made a promise to myself that I wouldn't touch her until she begged. That way, she couldn't deny her feelings, because when I finally walk her up the aisle, I want her to be happy about it and not feel forced in any way. But right now, as I look into her sleepy eyes, something draws me closer and then my lips are brushing hers. Lightly at first, until her hands grip my shirt, pulling me closer. She's hungry for the kiss, and her hands work their way up to my face and then into my hair. Her soft body is pressed so tightly against my own, I can feel her heartbeat against my chest. I pour everything into this kiss, trying to convey how I feel, until she pulls away gasping for breath.

She gives me a hungry look, like she can't wait to devour me. I wink, grabbing her by the hand and continuing to lead her up the hill. Once we get back to the house, I lead her straight up to our bedroom. Everyone else is in bed and the house is silent, but I still can't wait to be completely alone in the safety of the bedroom.

Chapter Ten

PIPER

I lie in bed with my mind racing. He kissed me and it felt amazing. Better than amazing. We walked back to the house hand-in-hand, but we never exchanged one word. We came straight to the bedroom because everyone else seemed to be in bed. And now, Anton is in the shower, and I'm laying here wondering what will happen next. Will he expect more from me? After our last encounter, which involved his hand in my underwear, I'm not convinced I have the willpower to turn him away.

I hear Mae's voice in my head telling me that I'm free and single, so what's stopping me? If I was to tell her that Hulk is stopping me, she'd slap me silly. Deep down, I know there's no future with Hulk, but it's hard to let go of a dream I've had since I was thirteen years old.

Anton enters the room wearing nothing but his shorts. I'm so used to seeing him in suits that I gawk at him like I've never seen a half-naked man before. He catches me staring and smirks. I watch him take a blanket and pillow from the wardrobe, then he goes over to the couch and lays everything out neatly. My heart sinks a little. After that kiss, I was expecting . . . well, I don't know what I was expecting, but I'm definitely disappointed when I see him climb under the blanket.

"Stop staring at me," he grumbles sleepily.

"Is the couch comfortable?" I ask.

"Probably not as comfy as that bed, but I'll survive. I don't need much sleep."

I lay back down and stare up at the sheer material that hangs across the top of the four-poster bed, twinkling lights wrapped within it. "Why?" I ask.

"I don't know. After around three or four hours, I just wake up."

"If I get anything less than eight hours, I'm a total cow."

"Good to know."

We fall silent, and I close my eyes. All I can picture is his naked chest. The skull tattoos that crawl up his abdomen. The way his back flexed as he straightened out his bedding. I shudder. "You know, we're both grown-ups. I'm sure we can share the bed without it being weird."

Anton doesn't answer me for some time, and I begin to think he's fallen asleep. "You think you can resist me?" he mumbles.

I smile to myself. "If you can resist me."

Anton gets up and pads across the room. He slips into bed beside me, lying on his stomach and stuffing his pillows underneath him. He wraps his muscled arms around the pillows, and I sigh, wishing I was them. I take the opportunity to look at the tattoos on his back. There are more skulls and entwined around them is a snake. "You like skulls a lot," I point out.

"One hundred forty-seven," he almost whispers. "There are one hundred forty-seven."

My hand hovers over the snake, and then, gently, I trace my finger over it. Anton's skin breaks out in pimples. "Why do you like them so much? And what's the snake all about?"

"The snake is my father." My hand stops. "He's crawling amongst the dead in hell."

"The skulls are how you envision hell?" I ask.

"The skulls stand for death, one for every man I've killed. And, yes, they're in hell where they belong. Where one day, we'll meet again."

"Oh," I mumble. I'm not shocked Anton has killed men, he's in the mob. He *is* the mob. "You think you'll go to hell?" I ask.

Anton rolls onto his back and catches my hand in his. "I know I will. The devil has a special place for me."

"What makes you so sure?" He laces his fingers with mine and rests our joined hands on his stomach.

"When you do as many bad things as I've done, you accept two things. One is that you'll most likely die younger than you would if you were a normal regular man. The second is that you'll pay for every sin in hell, an eternity of torture."

"And that didn't put you off?"

He smiles. "I can't wait to get there. I think I'll get more peace in hell than I've ever had on earth."

It saddens me that Anton feels this way. I move my head closer until it rests against his bulging bicep. "What would give you peace?"

I whisper. My eyes suddenly feel heavy with tiredness and a yawn escapes.

Anton kisses me on the head. "Death," he whispers back. "Now, sleep." As if his command is magic, my eyes close and I let sleep pull me under.

I wake with the sunshine warming my face. Blinking the sleep away, I look around the room to get my bearings. Anton isn't here, and I didn't hear him leave. On the bedside cabinet is a glass of orange juice. I smile and pull myself to sit up. I take the glass and groan with pleasure when the cool liquid hits my dry throat. On the stool at the end of the bed is a white bikini with a note attached saying, 'Wear me.' I smile wider, realising he's been in my bag. Then my eyes fall to the black box sitting neatly on Anton's pillow. It's the same box Anton put the vibrator in. It was in my bag because I didn't want my mum to go snooping and find it. Next to the box is a note saying, 'Use me.' I laugh out loud and flop back onto my pillow. Chewing on my lower lip,

ANTON

I stare at the box. I am alone, and it's been a while since I bothered to take care of myself.

I pull the lid from the box and take out the vibrator. I press the power button and it buzzes to life. It wouldn't hurt to relax and unwind. I am on holiday after all. Throwing the sheet back, I slip out of my panties eagerly, then I run my hand to my breast and close my eyes as I slide the vibrator between my parted legs.

The bedroom door suddenly swings open, and my eyes widen in horror. Anton stands in the doorway, frozen. In his hand is a tray laden with breakfast items. I squeal and release the vibrator so I can tug the sheet over myself. The purple plastic penis bounces on the mattress and drops to the floor with a thud. The vibrations sound so much louder on the wooden floor as it spins in a circle, and I cringe with embarrassment. Anton kicks the door closed behind him and places the tray on the end of the bed. He gracefully bends down and collects the toy from the floor.

"Don't move or you'll ruin your breakfast," he warns with a glint in his eye.

He bends to kiss me on the lips, remaining there while his hand travels along my stomach and between my legs. "Open your legs," he whispers against my lips. He runs the vibrating toy over my opening, and I buck against it, causing the breakfast tray to shake. He pulls it away, smirking. "Careful," he whispers. His intense stare and the low rumble of his voice is so hot, I'm ready to combust into a million pieces. He leans closer and kisses me, slow and gentle like last night. I'm taken to another world. One where I feel light and dreamy.

This time, when he presses the toy against me, I force myself to stay still. He rubs it back and forth a few times and then carefully slides it inside me. I inhale, my breath shaky. Anton turns the speed up and the pulses feel like they're vibrating all the way up my spine. "Do you need to come, Piper?" His words don't embarrass me like they should—I'm too far past that as I moan in pleasure. My body answers for me as I begin to shake and shudder, losing all control of my limbs. Waves crash over and over in the pit of my stomach as an orgasm rips me apart.

He pinches my nipple through the material of my shirt. It pulls another tremble from me, and I cry out. "Enjoy your breakfast," he murmurs, handing me the vibrator before turning on his heel and leaving the room.

I stare at the closed door and then down to the vibrator in my hand. Christ, what the fuck just happened? I let out a nervous laugh, flopping back onto the pillows before breaking out in a fit of giggles. Anton just fucked me with a toy, and I didn't hate it.

When I'm recovered, and my legs return to normal, I shower and dress in the bikini. I wrap myself in a pink caftan and pick up the now empty breakfast tray. A coffee and croissant were just what I needed to fill the hunger pangs brought on by such an intense orgasm.

I find everyone outside by the pool. The two men who came with us are Piero and Giovani. Apparently, both are capos, as Ella's kept me up to date with names and positions. They're sat in the shade, reading newspapers. Ella and Michael are talking by the outdoor bar, and Anton is lying face down on a sun lounger with a female rubbing cream into his back. She's clearly a member of staff as she's wearing the same blue uniform the other house staff wear, but a pinch of jealousy rears its ugly head regardless.

Anton rolls onto his front and thanks the woman, taking the cream from her. He spots me and gives a crooked smile, the kind that tells me he's thinking of our earlier interaction. My cheeks instantly heat, and I stare down at the ground. "Piper," he calls, forcing me to look up again. He holds the sun cream out at me, like that explains why he's shouting my name. When I stare blankly, he tips his head, asking me to go over.

As I reach him, he holds the cream out again. "Could you help me?"

"Apply cream that's already been applied?" I ask sarcastically.

He smirks. "Jealousy's a sexy colour on you." He snatches my wrist in his hand and tugs me to step closer. Then he takes me by the waist and lifts me to sit over his lap. "Make it look like we're at least a little in love," he whispers closer to my ear. I glance over at Piero and Giovani, who are watching us with interest. "They're forever watching," he adds, "checking up on me."

"Why?" I ask.

"Because they don't believe I'm in love."

"They haven't fallen for your lies?" I ask with a smirk.

He takes my hand and turns it palm up before squirting sun cream into it. He guides my hands together to share the lotion before placing them against his solid chest. I inhale sharply, shifting slightly. Anton immediately grips my hips and stills me as a small laugh escapes him. "Careful, bellissima, my head's full of memories of you coming and now you're rubbing against me in this," he plucks at the white strap on the top of my bikini, "sexy bikini. I'm not sure I can contain myself." He glances down between us, and my eyes follow, widening when they settle on his huge erection pushing to get free from his shorts. My cheeks burn red for a second time, and to distract myself, I move my hands in small circles, massaging the thick cream into his six-pack and then working up to his broad chest.

"You had some interesting items in your bag," he mutters, slipping his shades back over his eyes and placing his hands behind his head. He relaxes back while I continue to work my hands over him.

"You shouldn't go through my things."

"It was either me or Michael. I thought you'd prefer me, and I'm glad I did after what I found."

"You must be paranoid if you have to have your men check bags."

"It's surprising how many people want to kill me."

I grin. "Is it?" I ask, tipping my head to one side. I stand, moving over to the next sunbed. "My turn." I lie on my stomach, resting my head on my hands to look at him. When he doesn't move, I add, "Should I ask one of your men?"

He laughs. "You could, but they wouldn't dare touch you without my permission."

After a few seconds, he throws his legs over the edge of his sunbed and drags it closer to my own. He pulls the tie on my bikini top. "You don't want tan lines," he says, letting the strings fall open.

He squirts the cold cream onto my back and begins to rub it into my skin. I close my eyes and relax, enjoying the feel of him. When my back is done, he taps my shoulder, "Roll over," he tells me. I hold my bikini top in place and turn onto my back, letting the fabric rest over my breasts.

He begins to work the cream over my stomach, working his way up and slipping his hand under the top to cup my breast. I gasp, my eyes widening at his brazen attitude. "I could fuck you right now and they wouldn't bat an eyelid," he murmurs, tweaking my nipple. He moves his hand across to my other breast and repeats the action. "Now, fasten the top until I return," he tells me, standing and adjusting the tent in his shorts.

ANTON

I march through the house, fighting with myself not to drag Piper with me and fuck her senseless. The way her body reacts to me is an aphrodisiac, and I'm not ashamed to admit I'm already addicted.

Aurora is leaning against my office door sulkily. She's obsessed, and right now, that's enough for me to grab her by the hand and drag her upstairs. She giggles, and I'm about to go into my room when an image of Piper flashes through my mind, causing me to growl in frustration. I can't fuck another woman in the room I'm sharing with her. I pull Aurora farther down the hall to a spare room. I know she's not wearing underwear—she whispered it to me when she was rubbing cream into my back—so I pull her to sit over me, making quick work of opening my shorts.

I pull a condom from my pocket and rip it open, rolling it over my erection. "Rimuovi la parte superiore," I growl, and she lifts her shirt over her head and drops it to the floor. "Cavalcami," I order. She loves to ride me and wastes no time wrapping her hand around my cock and guiding me to her entrance. As she sinks onto me, she cries out, and I place my hand over her mouth. The last thing I need is to get caught with Aurora by Piero or Giovani.

"Sì, sì," her muffled cries shout against my palm. Her nails dig into my shoulder, and I relish the small amount of pain it causes. Aurora slaps my face hard, and I bite my lip by mistake. She sees the blood and grins. "Bastardo," she hisses and slaps me again.

I stand abruptly, and she wraps her legs around my waist. Laying her down on the edge of the bed, I place my hand around her throat, slamming into her fast and hard. Exactly how she likes it.

ANTON

I feel my orgasm building. "Devi venire," I hiss, telling her that she needs to come first. She tries to lash out at me again, but this time, I catch her hand and twist it down by her side. I force her onto her stomach and pull her arms behind her back. When I push my erection against the puckered hole of her arse, she squirms under me. It doesn't deter me, and I push forward. She screams out as her tight hole fights against my cock. Sweat trickles down my back as I begin to move in and out until she accepts me there.

This time, when my orgasm approaches, I let it come. My legs shake, and I growl into her hair as I ram into her backside, hard. As I shudder against her, she yells out again, and I feel the wetness of her ejaculation spread between our legs. With each thrust, she squirts a little more. I keep moving until she groans and shakes her head from side to side with exhaustion. "Non più," she moans over and over. *No more.*

I get back to the pool freshly showered and a lot more relaxed. Ella gives me an annoyed scowl. She knows what I've been up to. Having Aurora follow me out also freshly showered and with a rosy glow to her cheeks probably gave it away. Piper is unaware, still laying on her sun lounger as I pour myself a drink. "You're disgusting," Ella hisses. "Piper is right there."

I sigh. "Chill out, Els."

"I thought you liked Piper. You seemed to."

"I do," I say defensively, "but we're not together yet. Technically, I haven't done anything wrong."

Ella hops down from her bar stool. "So, you won't mind if I go over there and tell her?" I grip her by the arm, and she glowers at me. "What's the problem if you aren't together?" she asks, arching her brow.

"There are two types of women, Ella. Ones that you fuck on the side because they let you play out your fantasies, and ones you make love to and marry. The latter carry your heir and complete your life."

Ella huffs and shakes her head with disappointment. "You sound just like him," she mutters. "Just like Dad." My blood runs cold. My eyes narrow, and Ella steps back from me. She senses the anger rising. "It's the truth," she snaps. "What kind of woman will I be to someone? The whore or the wife?"

"This isn't about you," I growl.

"Well, you're saying there are only two kinds of women. Dad thought I was the whore. He could live out his fantasies through me—"I slam my hand on the bar, and she presses her lips closed into a tight line. I feel everyone's eyes on us.

"Remove yourself from my sight before I lose it," I warn, and she wastes no time rushing off inside. I knock my drink back in one and refill my glass. A second passes before I hear Piper padding towards me. I keep my back to her. She runs a hand over my shoulder, her fingers stopping on the nail marks that Aurora left there.

"Everything okay?" she asks. I nod, bowing my head and resting my hands against the bar edge. There's an uncomfortable feeling swirling in the pit of my stomach. It's not something I've ever felt before, and I wonder if this is what guilt might feel like. "Do you want to talk about it?"

Piper places both hands on either shoulder and begins to rub my tired muscles. It feels good, but having her innocent, delicate hands trying to rub away the guilt and stress makes me feel even worse, so I shrug her off. "I just need five goddamn minutes without you fucking women wanting to talk about feelings," I yell.

My shortness has the desired effect because I feel her step back. "I was trying to help. There's no need to yell like that."

I spin to face her and see the hurt in her expression. My heart aches with guilt, and I rub it subconsciously. "Who the fuck do you think you're talking to?" I hiss, keeping my voice dangerously low.

Piper glances across the pool to where Michael and the other two men sit. When she sees they aren't coming to intervene, she narrows her eyes at me. "Does that work? Yell, and the world does what you want?" she asks. "It's rude. If you didn't want my help, you just had to say."

"I've killed men for talking back to me," I warn.

ANTON

"I'm not scared of you," she mutters, squaring her tiny shoulders and jutting out her chin.

"Well, you should be!"

"You try and lay one finger on me, and I will slit your damn throat in your sleep," she advises me.

"You ever slit a man's throat before, Piper?" I smirk, moving closer to her. "Because I have and it's a messy job. I won't die straightaway. You'll have to look into my eyes as I gargle and choke on my own blood. I'll thrash about, trying to suck air into my deflating lungs."

She narrows her eyes. "It'll be an experience, for sure."

"I'm going to enjoy breaking you, Piper." I smile. "I like a challenge." I walk around her and head inside. Her feisty attitude is turning me on, and I need to put distance between us.

One thing I've learned about Piper is the more I pull away, the more she's intrigued.

Chapter Eleven

PIPER

I flop onto the bed and press my mobile back to my ear. I decided to call Mae so I could talk through the confusion I'm currently feeling when it comes to Anton. Part of me hates him. He blackmailed me to step into his life, and I should be angry. But occasionally, I see another side to him and I like it.

"I'm weird, right?"

She laughs. "No, Piper, you're normal. I'd be lying if I said I didn't get a kick out of pissing Ace off every now and then. Make-up sex is amazing."

I screw my face up even though she can't see me. "Really? What about when he's being horrible?"

ANTON

"It's not often Ace is intentionally horrible. I mean, not to me anyway. And if he is, like if he snaps at me, I usually know it's for a reason, like he's stressing over something. Most of the time, he apologises once he's calmed down. I think we're all a little like that sometimes." She sighs. "I wish he would yell at me right now. It'd be better than him treating me like a broken China doll."

I groan out loud. "Sorry, Mae. I shouldn't be bothering you with my stupid problems right now."

"Don't you dare hang up," she yells. "I need this right now. It's boring sitting here, worrying about my own woes. Besides, your problems amuse me."

I smile into the phone. "Trust you to find amusement in my pain."

"Look, you like him. Why are you overthinking this? He's going to come with issues. Like Ace, he has a lot on his shoulders. But that doesn't mean I think you should lie down and let him walk all over you, because that's not your style. Treat him how you treat The Rebellion when they speak like crap to you. But then enjoy making up with him." She giggles, and I realise how much I've missed that sound.

"Thanks, Mae. I love you."

"I know you do," she says confidently.

"How is he?" I ask, and she knows I'm talking about Hulk because it's a habit I can't seem to break.

"He's Hulk. Annoying, abrupt, drinking too much, and fucking everything that looks in his pathetic direction," she says, and I sigh. "If it's any consolation, I think he's hurting over you, and he's all over the place right now. I don't understand why he pushes you away and then plays the wounded victim when you reject him."

"I don't think about him as much as I used to. Does it mean I'm falling out of love with him?" I ask, sadness squeezing my heart.

Mae goes silent for a second, processing my words. "Maybe. It's been a long time coming. I've been praying for the day that you'd wake up and see he isn't good enough for you."

"But you think Anton is?" I ask.

"No," she says honestly, "but I think he'll help heal you so that you can one day find a man who is. And let's face it, Anton's spoiling you like a man should spoil his woman." My heart gives another squeeze, because Anton isn't my man. Not really.

The bedroom door opens, and Anton marches in and heads straight for the bathroom. "I have to go, Mae. I'll call you again soon."

"Stay strong. Be badass," she says. "Speak soon."

I disconnect the call. Anton's left the bathroom door ajar, and I resist the urge to peek through the small gap to catch a glimpse. "I have to visit someone," he shouts from the shower. "When I return, we have plans, so be ready for eight o'clock." I roll my eyes and open a social media app on my mobile phone. "Are you listening to me?" he asks, but I remain silent. Mae's right, he needs to know it's not okay to talk to me like shit.

The shower turns off as I continue to scroll through my social media. I hear his footfalls enter the bedroom. "Piper," he growls. When I ignore him again, he moves into my line of vision. "Are you trying to make me mad?" He waits for a beat for my reply and then snatches my mobile from my hand and throws it beside me on the bed. "It's a party. I'll lay your clothes out," he continues.

I follow him with my eyes as he goes into the walk-in wardrobe. I noticed a few dresses hanging in there earlier, all new with tags on and, not surprisingly, all in my size. He returns with a short white dress. It'll enhance my tanned skin, but I already know I won't wear it. He seems to read my mind and pushes his face closer to my own. Grabbing my chin between his thumb and forefinger, he forces me to look into his blazing eyes.

"Don't even think of wearing anything other than that dress. Nothing but that dress. If you do, I'll strip you naked in front of everyone." It's a warning that I'm pretty sure he'll carry out. *If he wants me to wear nothing but that dress, that's exactly what he'll get.*

He keeps his face in mine. Our breaths hitch and something changes between us. I feel like electricity is rushing from his fingertips and entering my body where we're connected. Aggressively, he pushes his lips against mine. The kiss is angry and hard. His well-trimmed beard rubs against my face, causing a burning sensation, and I welcome it. I pull myself into a kneeling position, and he pushes his hands into my hair, not breaking the kiss.

I eventually break away, and we stare at each other, panting. His hands are still gripping my hair at the base of my neck, and he pulls me back to him for another hungry kiss. My stupid stubbornness is now melting away as I run my hands over his broad shoulders. I feel the nail marks again and wonder if I did that to him this morning when he brought me to orgasm using the toy. I smile against his lips at the memory.

Anton's hands move to my shoulders and then to the string of my bikini top. He tugs it open, and the top falls away, leaving me bare to him. He pulls back and his eyes feast upon my naked breasts. His hands cover them and he rubs his thumbs over my nipples. Leaning down, he takes one in his mouth. The warmth of his tongue causes sensations deep in my pussy and I groan out loud, unashamed of my wanton behaviour as I grip his head to my breast.

Suddenly, Anton steps back. He glares at me, his breaths coming out as pants and his chest heaving like he's just run a marathon. His erection is practically bursting through the towel that hangs tightly around his waist. "I have to go," he mutters, stepping back again.

"Are you kidding me?" I snap angrily.

"That dress or you'll pay the price," he mutters, pointing at the white garment on the bed. I watch open-mouthed as he goes back into the bathroom, this time closing the door firmly.

I remain on my knees on the bed, wondering what the hell just happened. How can a man keep stroking the fire only to walk away before he's had his release? That's the third time he's been intimate with me, only to leave me before he's taken what he needs. It makes no sense.

I get into bed. All the heat and emotional torment is taking its toll. I must fall asleep because I don't hear Anton leave, but when I next open my eyes, he's gone. I reach for my mobile and see it's now seven in the evening. Groaning, I take myself to have a shower so I can get ready for another night of confusion with Mr. Jekyll and Hyde himself.

When I emerge from the bedroom at seven forty-five, I feel amazing. Gone is the unsure and wanton hoe from this afternoon, and in her place is a confident female who is ready to deal with Anton's bullshit.

ANTON

I enter the kitchen and find Ella dressed in a stunning summer dress. Her long black hair is curled into loose waves, and she has a minimal amount of makeup applied that enhances the dewy glow of her naturally dark skin. I've never seen her dressed up and wearing makeup. She's beautiful. She catches me staring and blushes. "Thought I'd make the effort seeing as my brother is forcing me to come to this stupid party."

"Well, you look really nice, Ella," I say sincerely, and she smiles. "And if at any point you feel overwhelmed, just let me know and we'll go out together and get air." She nods in appreciation. I don't know Ella's exact circumstances, but from what the guys have said back at the club, she suffered at the hands of her father.

The air changes when Anton steps into the room. He goes to Ella and kisses her on each cheek. "I apologise for earlier," he says quietly to her. "Thank you for coming this evening. I know how hard this will be for you."

She smiles at him. "I'm sorry too. It's because I care." Anton kisses her again, this time on her head, and shrugs into his suit jacket. "Michael is waiting out front. Let's go." He passes me without even a sideways glance, and I can't deny that it hurts my heart a little.

Ella reaches for my hand and gives it a gentle squeeze. "It'll be okay," she whispers.

Michael drives us to another large villa. The front of the building is illuminated with spotlights, giving it an inviting glow. We follow Anton and Michael up the steps, and when the door opens, a butler greets us, bowing his head as we enter. He leads us through the house, which is just as grand as the place we're staying in. We're taken out back, where the large garden space is buzzing with life. Anton takes my hand firmly. He must sense that I'm reluctant, so he squeezes tighter, preventing me from pulling away. He leads me through the throngs of people, stopping several times for guests to kiss his hand like he's God. It's a strange sight to behold.

We get to a patio area with some unoccupied seats. Anton pulls one out for me, and I sit carefully. The dress is pretty short, and I'm beginning to think my plan has backfired as I tug

ANTON

the hem down as much as I can. When Anton sits next to me, he runs his index finger along my exposed thigh. "You wore the dress," he whispers, leaning in close. I stare ahead blankly. "Wise choice," he adds, smirking.

"Just the dress," I quip, pissed at his ability to annoy me with just a smirk.

He gives me a quizzical look and then it dawns on him what I'm saying. His eyes dart to the various parts of me that would normally be covered with underwear. The dress is double layered, and I checked nothing could be seen through the material, but I see him assessing to make sure. Now, I smirk and tug at the top of the dress that already hangs low across my breasts, exposing a little more.

"Do you know how important this evening is?" he growls. "And you think it's acceptable to come here and behave like a whore?"

I bite the inside of my lower lip to stop me from reacting to his insult. "You said I should wear nothing but the dress. I was following your orders, master, as you requested." I bat my eyelashes innocently, and he looks fit to burst.

"So, you thought you'd get back at me by playing your little game because I was specific in what you wear?"

"I don't like being told what to wear."

"You're playing a part. Tonight's about my capo, Luke, who died. This is a celebration of his life. His mother specifically requested that the women wear light colours and the men wear suits."

I glance around at the guests and briefly close my eyes. A lump forms in my throat, and suddenly, I feel like there's not enough air. I'm saved as an elder woman approaches us, taking Anton's attention away from me. He stands and leans over the table to kiss her cheeks. He reaches to my hand while the woman is hugging him and pulls me to stand. He speaks Italian, but I know he is introducing me because I hear my name.

The woman kisses my cheeks and speaks to me in Italian. "She says you're very beautiful," Anton interprets, his expression blank. "But, of course, she doesn't know you're pantiless at her son's celebration of life," he adds, cocking his eyebrow. My cheeks flush, and I pray that she doesn't understand any English.

The woman grasps both my hands in hers and begins chatting animatedly. "She says she gets good feelings about you. She knows you'll be in my life forever," says Anton. I scoff, and he scowls at me. "She says there will be times that you are angry with me, but you are a good thing in my life and you have to stick with me through the rough times. The good times will be worth it."

I narrow my eyes in his direction. "You're making this up," I mutter.

Anton laughs. "I swear, I'm not. Maria can see into the future."

Maria guides my face back to look at her. I feel like I'm under real scrutiny as her eyes pierce mine. I've never believed in this sort of thing, but she stares so intently that it's hard not to. She begins talking, but this time, she's looking at Anton as she speaks. He bows his head as she talks to him. "What's she saying now?" I ask. Maria shakes her head at him like she is disappointed, and his eyes are filled with an emotion I'm used to seeing in men. It's guilt.

"Nothing. It's about her son." I know it's a lie, and I commit that look to memory, so the next time he lies, I recognise it.

"You'll give me a son," he adds, his eyes fixed on Maria. "Soon."

I laugh and shake my head. "Now, I know you're making this up. Can she feel that we're fake news?"

"Is the sexual chemistry flying between us fake news?" he quips. "No one said you had to be in a relationship with me to give me a son." I screw my face up. There's not a chance in hell I'll have a child with Anton Martinez. I get daily whiplash from his moods as it is. Spending my life raising his child would be torture.

Ella joins us, and thankfully, Maria's attention is drawn to her. They embrace, and when Maria begins talking to Ella, tears fill her eyes. They wander away together, and I'm left alone once again with Anton.

"If you're going to be the mother of my children, you'd better dress appropriately," he quips, sitting back in his chair. I snatch a glass of something clear and bubbly from a passing waitress.

"Maria is wrong," I say firmly. "I wasn't prepared to bring a child up alone with Hulk and I'm not going to do it for you."

ANTON

Anton laughs. "If you think you'll be aborting my child, then you're wrong. I'll lock you up until the child is born."

"And force me to raise it?" I snap.

"Once the child is born, I won't have a need for you."

I almost choke on my drink. "So, you'd get your kid and then dispose of me like a piece of rubbish?"

"Or you could live a happy life by my side, raising my children. It's your choice." This conversation suddenly feels very real, almost like he's confirming this is our future.

I force a laugh, but he doesn't join me. "Why do I feel like I'm having a conversation about something you've already decided?"

"You knew I wanted something from you, Piper."

My eyes widen and I lean closer. "A few dates is what you said, Anton, not a fucking family," I hiss.

"Careful, Piper, let's not take the attention away from the purpose of the night."

I glower at him, folding my arms across my chest. "We are not having sex, Anton. I will not have your child."

ANTON

I let Piper have her tantrum. Pulling her up on the way she's acting will only cause it to get heated, taking the attention away from why we're all here. "I don't know why you think you're calling the shots when I hold all the cards."

"This ends tonight," she mutters, staring out across the guests. "I don't want any of this. I did what you asked and attended a few dates, now I want to go back to my normal life and—"

"Hulk?" I cut in. "Your normal life with Hulk? Is that why you thought I'd like this," I point to her dress, "no underwear bullshit? He treats you like a whore, and you dress like one?"

She balls her fists at her sides, her face red with rage. "He loves me in his own way. And you're hardly treating me any better."

I scoff, rolling my eyes. "I bring you to my home in Italy. I introduce you to my family and friends. I give you two orgasms without taking anything for myself, and you think I'm treating you badly?"

ANTON

She drinks the glass of Champagne like water, not even wincing as the bubbles go down. "You blackmailed me to be here."

"Which is exactly why I get to tell you when we're done. And in case you didn't get the message," he leans closer, "we're *not* done."

"You wanted your men to see you with the same piece of arse more that once. Now, they have, so the job's done."

Her glass is replaced for a third time, and I shake my head at the waitress to indicate she won't need any more. "Think about it," I say. "Where are you more likely to be happiest? With me, playing the part of a pampered princess, or at the clubhouse with Hulk, hating you after he finds out you aborted his child without telling him and your father looking at you like a piece of shit because you danced like a call girl in my club?" She snatches up her glass and rises to her feet. I tug her dress lower at the back. It barely covers her arse cheeks, and I'm regretting my decision to not lay down more specific guidelines. "Where are you going?"

"Away from you," she retorts, walking away.

I snigger as Michael fills the vacated chair. "Going well?"

"I need to marry her while she's here in Italy," I say, and Michael's eyes widen in shock. "Maria saw her carrying my son."

Michael rolls his eyes. "Maria is grieving her own son, and she's probably had too many sambucas."

I shake my head, my eyes fixed on Piper's rounded arse as she leans over the bar to speak to the waiter. "No. She knew I'd cheated. She said if I wasn't careful, I'd lose Piper, and she'd take my son away."

"Listen to yourself. Piper isn't even yours, and you're talking like she's pregnant. Maria is crazy. And who the hell have you hooked up with?"

"Aurora," I admit on a sigh, and Michael slaps me on the shoulder, laughing. "It was a mistake. One I won't repeat."

"It's not cheating when you and Piper aren't real."

I knock my drink back. He might be right, but I still felt guilty for it. "Invite Alberto and his brothers to the house tomorrow evening. He's going to marry us."

Michael frowns. "Anton, you're acting crazy. She'll never agree to that, and are you actually saying you want to be tied to this woman forever because of some bullshit that Maria made up?"

I nod. "She won't think the marriage is real until it's done. I have a plan. Tell Alberto I'll brief him when he arrives."

Michael murmurs something in Italian under his breath. "As your advisor, I'm making it clear I think this is a bad decision. If," he sighs, "*when* this goes wrong, you'll have to give the order for her to disappear. Are you strong enough for that?"

"It won't go wrong. Call Alberto."

He shakes his head, a laugh escaping him. "You and Tag have done some crazy shit, but this, it tops it all."

I stand, fastening my jacket and scanning the room for Piper. I catch her disappearing down into the garden. The more time I spend with her, the more I need. Maria saw what I've been dreaming of, and I need to make it my reality, but I can only do that if I show Piper I'm worth being with. The games have to come to an end.

Chapter Twelve

♥

PIPER

I sit on the small stone wall and stare out over the skyline. The beautiful thing about Italy is the hills allow you to see for miles, and tonight, I'm treated to the sun slowly setting, making the sky a hazy orange colour.

A man sits beside me, smiling wide. "I was watching you," he says, his Italian accent thick. "You're very beautiful." I arch a brow as he runs his finger over my knee. The men here seem to be attracted to my pale skin like flies to shit.

"I wouldn't do that if I were you," I begin, but it's too late as Anton reaches over my head and grips the man's finger, pulling it back until it makes a sickening snap sound. I wince as the man howls in pain. Anton shoves a handkerchief into the man's open mouth, muffling his cries. He hisses something in Italian into his ear and the man stops his noise.

Another man rushes over, looking panic-stricken. "Mr. Martinez, I am so sorry. I'll have him removed right away." His words are rushed as he clicks his fingers in the air rapidly. "He's only been with us for a short time. He isn't made yet." I watch as the man is led away holding his finger.

Anton turns his anger to the apologetic man. "If he isn't a made man, why is he here?" The man visibly shrinks back but wisely chooses to remain silent. "Maybe I should pay you a visit tomorrow and make sure your organisation is in order?"

The man bows his head. "You are welcome anytime, Mr. Martinez."

Anton takes my hand and pulls me to stand, then he marches back towards the house, tugging me along behind. "Anton," I hiss, trying to pull free. He grips harder, leading us out the front door and around to the side of the house. He releases me, turning quickly and taking me by surprise. Without a word, he steps closer until I'm backed against the wall. His eyes search my face, for what I'm unsure, and after a few seconds, he slams his lips against mine in a bruising kiss, not stopping until he's stolen every last breath and I'm left panting with need.

His stare only intensifies, then he tucks my hair away from my face before whispering, "You're mine." His moods are so confusing, much like Hulk's, and I smirk at how similar they are. "I can't stop thinking about you being naked under this," he adds, plucking at the dress.

"You want to see?" I tease, grinning and taking the hem between my fingers. It works—he grins, and I relax a little. I like this version of him, the one I can joke around with. He hooks his finger in the top of the dress and tugs it an inch from my body, peering down at my breasts, and I laugh. "Perv," I add.

His mouth is close again, and I stare longingly. All this teasing is driving me insane, so I take the plunge and gently press my lips against his. I pause, hoping he doesn't pull away. It's the first time I've been daring enough to make the first move. He smiles, taking my face in his hands and sweeping his tongue into my mouth.

ANTON

It's slow and sexy, making my toes curl. "You push all the boundaries," he murmurs, resting his forehead against mine. "It's addictive."

His words stir something inside me and, for a moment, it's possible to see a future for us, together. I wrap my arms around his neck and pull him in for another kiss. This time, it's desperate and rushed. Our teeth clash and his hands run down my body. He lifts me, trapping me between him and the wall, and I wrap my legs around his waist. My dress has risen, exposing my naked lower half, and he pushes his hand between us, running a finger through my folds. I hum my approval, and he growls, quickly unfastening his belt and unzipping his trousers. He shoves them halfway down his thighs and enters me in one swift motion. I cry out in surprise, and he kisses me again to steal the sound. I'm vaguely aware there's no barrier between us, but he's moving so fast, the pleasure is rolling through me before I can process it all.

Clinging to his shoulders, I hold on for dear life as he slams into me, grunting with exertion. I come apart quickly, shuddering until my body turns to mush and I'm left whimpering. Anton pulls from me, taking his erection in his hand and moving his fist back and forth. I lower to my hunches, and he groans, watching through hooded eyes as I swipe my tongue over the swollen head of his cock. I taste myself mixed with him and open wider, letting him slide between my lips. He presses his hands against the wall, keeping his eyes fixed on me as I suck him. After a few minutes, he stills, tensing and muttering words in Italian. I feel his cock swell and then streams of cum hit the back of my throat. I take everything, wincing as I swallow the bitter taste down.

He rests his head against the wall, closing his eyes while he gathers himself. I slip under his arm and move away, straightening my dress and running my fingers through my hair. I'm not sure how to feel about having sex with Anton. We've spent days teasing one another, and finally, we gave in. I glance his way, and he's stuffing himself back into his trousers. He catches me watching and smiles. "Are you okay?" he asks. I smile too, nodding. Something's changed between us.

He takes my hand and pulls me to him, placing a kiss on my head. "Go and wait in the car.

I'll say my goodbyes, and we'll go home. I have plans for us tomorrow."

ANTON

Piper was exhausted when we arrived home and went straight to bed. I promised to follow, yet here I am, sitting by the pool alone, thinking over my plans. Minutes pass and Michael arrives, stopping by the bar to fill a glass before joining me. "Where did you rush off to?" he asks.

"Piper was tired," I reply, not bothering to look at him.

I feel him assessing me. "You fucked her," he says, sounding amused.

"Do you have to be so crude?" I snap, scowling.

He laughs again. "Careful, you sound like you're catching feelings, boss."

I sigh heavily, swirling the ice in my drink. "I don't know what the fuck's happening," I admit. "It's gone way beyond what I imagined. I'm making reasons to tie her to me."

"Yah know, you could just do it the old fashioned way," he suggests, and I bring my eyes to his. He shrugs. "Date her, fall in love, marry her, have children."

I shake my head. "She's only here because I forced her to be. I've blackmailed her into this, and now, I'm . . ." I groan. "I'm scared she'll leave."

Michael gives me a sympathetic look. "Maybe she won't. Ask her out properly."

"And if she says no? If she tells me she still loves that fuck-up biker, then what?"

He shrugs again. "You find someone else."

I scowl, hating the idea. "It's too late, I want her."

He knocks his drink back. "Then we stick to the plan and tie her to you, so she can't walk away." He clinks his now empty glass against my own. "Exactly how are we doing that again?"

"By making her think Alberto is as crazy as Maria," I mutter, already feeling guilty. "Maybe getting her drunk so she doesn't realise?"

He sniggers. "I don't think that'll work, but I'm game for anything. You realise that you'll need to consummate the marriage or she can annul it."

I nod. The whole reason I'd spent the last few days teasing her was so, on our wedding night, we could consummate the whole thing. But tonight, I lost control, and now, I know for certain I can't let her walk away.

I spend the rest of the night sitting beside Piper while she sleeps, occasionally stroking her hair and whispering apologies. Tricking her is a low move, but I won't risk her going back to Hulk.

When the sun rises, I've decided on a relaxing day by the pool. I've even hired a bartender to make cocktails, telling myself it's something she'll enjoy rather than admitting it's part of my plan to get her so intoxicated, she can't figure out what I'm doing.

Piper and Ella are relaxing by the pool, sipping their first cocktails of the day. Aurora follows me into the kitchen. She runs her hand over my shoulder and smiles seductively. I shake my head and still her hand. "Not today, Aurora," I say in Italian, and she pouts. She's a hard habit to break, but if I'm serious about Piper, I can't go there again.

We've been hooking up since I was sixteen. She's always here when I return to Italy because her family works for mine. I decide to tell her I'm marrying Piper, so she doesn't get any ideas of flirting in front of her. She leaves the room, muttering that I'm an ass, and I let her have that. She's pissed, but I don't want to cause a scene and bring any attention from Piper.

I head back out to the pool and find Ella is now taking a swim. I steal her chair and take Piper by the hand. She eyes the connection, and I smirk, lying back and closing my eyes. "What?" I ask.

"You're acting weird."

"I'm not acting, Piper. Not anymore." I glance her way before slipping my shades on. "Last night was perfect," I add.

"Are you telling me you like me, Anton?" she asks, laughing.

I frown. "Would that be so weird?"

She falls silent for a few minutes before stating, "I just . . . well, it's all been a bit sudden and I—"

ANTON

I squeeze her hand gently. "Shh, let's not ruin the moment," I mutter. But she's confirmed my fears—she's not ready to forget Hulk, and I'm not ready to let her go, so my plan will go ahead.

By the time Alberto arrives with his brothers, the girls are giggly from the cocktails. I encourage them to dress for the evening, promising them food and more alcohol.

While they're gone, the cook starts up the barbeque and a few of my capos arrive. I only need a handful to witness my marriage so the word spreads, and by inviting a close few, they feel special, which means they're more likely to approve of me marrying a British woman over an Italian.

We eat and drink some more. Alberto is eccentric, and Piper instantly warms to him. I pull him to one side to check that he's set to go. I owe him big for all his trouble today. Not only has he managed to get the paperwork approved so an official ceremony can take place, but he's also willing to push this wedding through without seeing any of Piper's documents, apart from her passport. It's surprising what money and power can buy at such short notice.

We re-join Piper and Michael, who are deep in conversation. I pull her closer and wrap my arm around her shoulder. "Alberto thinks you're amazing," I tell her with a smile.

"Only because I can out-drink him," she replies.

"I give you a bet," says Alberto in his broken English. Up until now, he'd been letting her win every drinking challenge. He lays a pack of cards on the table. "I need practice to wedding," he says, and Piper looks at me confused.

"He's a civil registrar," I explain. "His first wedding is tomorrow and he's nervous," I lie.

"The first to turn ace card win. If you win, I give you one hundred euros. I win, I practice on you and Mr. Martinez."

"Why does he do everything with a game?" she asks me.

"Amuse him," I say. "Make the old boy happy."

ANTON

"Fine." She turns the first card and it's an ace. Alberto mocks a pain in his chest and hands over one hundred euros. "Again," he says, shuffling the cards. They take turns until Alberto turns over an ace and he jumps up excitedly. "I marry you," he says.

"You practice," corrects Piper, and he waves his hand around, dismissing her.

"Come," he says, taking her hand. He orders everyone to bring a chair and sit near the decked area.

Piper looks at me. "Talk about weird," she mutters.

"But look how happy he is," I point out, and she smiles.

Once everyone is seated, Alberto leads me to the front of the decked area. He then orders Michael to stand at the end of his makeshift altar with Piper. Ella approaches me. "Tell me this isn't what I think it is," she hisses.

"Aww, come on, sis. You said you like Piper."

"You can't trick someone into marrying you," she snaps.

"Sit down, Ella. This is important, and it's going to happen. You step one foot out of line and I'll have you removed." My warning is low and firm, and she knows I won't stand for any nonsense.

"I can't believe you're doing this. Why can't you just be normal and date, then ask her properly?"

"Because I want it now."

Ella shakes her head, her expression full of disappointment. "You never could wait for anything." She marches back to her seat, slumping down with her arms folded across her chest like a stropping teenager.

Alberto makes his way back to the front. Once he's in place, he presses play on his iPod and some classical music begins to play softly in the background. He gives Michael a nod, and Piper hooks her arm into his. They slowly walk down the centre. Piper giggles most of the way, and when she reaches me, Michael places a kiss on her cheek and steps away. "This is like a real wedding," she whispers, wobbling on unsteady feet.

Alberto begins the ceremony, pausing a few times to make it look like he's forgotten his lines. Piper occasionally tells him how fantastic he's doing, even though he's speaking in Italian and she doesn't understand a word he's saying.

ANTON

He asks if anyone knows of any lawful reason why we should not be married. I give Ella a warning glance, breathing a sigh of relief when Alberto moves on. "Ora ti pronuncio marito e moglie." He smiles, and everyone claps. "I pronounce you husband and wife," he translates for Piper. "You may kiss," he adds.

I swoop in for a kiss, tilting her back and making a show of it. She laughs and hits me playfully on the chest.

She kisses Alberto on the cheek. "You did very well, Alberto. You'll do fine tomorrow." He pats her hand and nods. When she looks away, he indicates that I should follow him.

We go to my office with Michael, and Alberto opens the register and signs his name. I sign my own and Piper's, and Michael signs as the witness. Alberto then writes out the marriage certificate, and once it's all done, I hand him a thick envelope of cash. He shakes my hand gratefully and goes to collect his brothers so they can leave.

Chapter Thirteen

PIPER

Rolling onto my back, I groan, covering my eyes with my arm. The light is too bright, and my head is pounding. My mouth is so dry that my tongue sticks to the roof of my mouth.

I try to sit up, but that only makes my head hurt more, so I flop back onto my pillow. The door opens and Anton enters. He holds out a glass of water, and I take it gratefully. "Those cocktails seemed like a good idea at the time," I groan, sitting to gulp the water. "Tell me Ella is suffering too."

"She's used to the strength of the drinks here. Plus, she didn't play shot games."

I groan again. "Oh god, I forgot about that."

"We fly home this evening. Get some food and water. You'll be fine in no time."

It's almost midnight when we land in London. I slept on the plane, so my hangover has finally disappeared. We make the hour drive towards home and as Michael turns on Anton's road, I turn to him and say, "Actually, I thought I could go home."

"It's late. I'll take you tomorrow." Anton's expression tells me there's no point arguing, his decision is final.

I turn on my mobile and it beeps immediately, indicating I have messages. The first is from Mae, telling me she misses me and can't wait to see me. I scroll to the next, which is from Hulk.

Hulk: I miss you. I hate not being able to come to your room in the middle of the night so you can fuck my nightmares away.

I roll my eyes and shake my head in irritation. The only thing he misses is his booty call.

"Who's texted you?" asks Anton.

"Mae and Hulk," I say.

Anton reaches over, plucking my mobile from my hands. I protest, but he ignores me, flicking through the messages and narrowing his eyes when he reads the one from Hulk. "He was drunk," I explain. "It happens when he's drunk."

"Now you're gonna defend him?"

"I'm just saying that he doesn't mean anything by it. He's had too much to drink."

"And if I was to drop you home, would you act on this text?" he asks, glaring at me.

"No. Of course not."

"But you let him kiss you right outside my house, so how do I know you wouldn't give in to him?" The car arrives at the house and Michael gets out to open my door. Anton grabs my hand, stopping me from exiting. "Well?"

I pull free and escape the vehicle. He follows. "I'm getting whiplash from your mood swings," I mutter, rushing up the steps. The door opens and I push past the staff member. "Why do you care anyway? Don't you think it's time we went back to our own lives?" I head upstairs, taking them two at a time, but he's hot on my heels.

"No, I don't," he snaps, grabbing my hand before I can enter the spare room. He guides me to his room.

"What are you doing?" I ask, tugging my arm free. Anton pushes his door open and I stare open-mouthed. Inside, candles decorate the entire room. The flames flicker and the shadows on the walls look like they're dancing. Red rose petals stand out against the white bedsheets, and I gasp. It's beautiful.

"Piper, I wanted our first time to be like you imagined your real first time to be. The candles, the rose petals. But then, I lost control and," he pauses, "well, you know how that ended. So, I wanted to make it up to you."

"You remembered what I said?" I whisper, hardly daring to believe he listened to the details I spewed out weeks ago. No one's ever done anything so romantic for me.

"Of course, mia amata. *My love*." He gently moves my hair over my shoulder and reaches for the first button on my shirt. "I wanted a chance to put it right. Screwing you against a wall outdoors wasn't how I wanted things to go between us." He presses his lips against mine and takes his time. This is a different kind of kiss to how we usually kiss. It's gentle and slow.

My mind races. When he takes what he wants from me, I don't usually have time to think. My body reacts and I lose control, but when he's gentle like this, I think of all the reasons we shouldn't do this again. "Relax," he whispers against my lips.

"I can't. You're giving me too much thinking time," I say. He smiles and pushes my top from my shoulders until it falls to the floor. He unfastens my jeans and pushes them down my legs for me to step out of them. "I'm not sure this is a good idea," I mutter "A second ago, you were mad with me."

He walks me backward until my legs hit the edge of the bed and I sit down. "I'm still mad," he says, kissing my cheek and nipping along my jaw. I close my eyes, trying to fight the butterflies he's causing in my stomach. "But this needs to happen," he adds. I frown, but before I can question him, he pushes me to lie down and parts my legs. Running his mouth along my inner thigh, he drags his warm tongue along my skin until he's between my legs.

ANTON

He pulls my underwear to one side and slides a finger into me. "Your smell drives me insane," he growls, licking along my opening. I buck off the bed. "And you taste even better." He buries his mouth against me, sucking, licking, and biting, giving me no time to process before I'm coming apart. I'm still trying to catch my breath and gather my thoughts when he flips me over and places his erection at my entrance.

"You're addictive," he pants, entering me. He pushes me down into the bed and fucks me. I cling to the mattress to stop myself shifting up the bed as he pounds into me. "We could have this all the time," he adds, "if you'd just forget about him." He moves faster still, digging his fingers into my waist. "I had no choice but to make you mine, Piper, you have to believe that."

I frown. "What are you talking about?"

He growls, stilling as his orgasm builds. "Fuck," he pants, shaking.

"Anton," I hiss, "you didn't use a condom." I try to wriggle away, but he holds me there, slowly moving back and forth as he releases into me.

I lay still, lying my head against the mattress and glaring at the wall. He pulls from me, and I feel our wetness coating my thighs. Anton runs his hand up my leg, and I try to shove him away. He pins me to the mattress again and rubs our juices into my skin like he's marking me.

When he's satisfied, he lets go of me and heads towards the bathroom without a word. I push to sit and look around the room. It felt so romantic moments ago, and now, it feels cheap and dirty. I brush away some of the rose petals in distain. "What the fuck was that?"

"Sex," he says, and I hear the shower running. "Isn't that how you like it with Hulk?"

I roll my eyes. "We're back to that?"

"A fucking cheap text is all it takes, right, Piper? I treat you like a queen, fly you to Italy, hire cocktail waiters to serve you . . . I even make your first time a fucking reality, but he sends you a booty call and your eyes light up."

I push up from the bed and go into the bathroom, where steam billows from the shower. "That's not true. You're making shit up so you can be angry. When we started this whole thing, you said it would help me win Hulk back. It's what you wanted."

"Because I knew it's what you wanted."

"Well, I don't want it," I shout. "Not anymore." I frown, realising my words are true. I don't want Hulk.

"It's too late for you and him anyway," Anton mutters, turning his back to me and rinsing soap from his body.

"What did you mean?" I ask, feeling uneasy. "When you said you had no choice but to make me yours?"

"The file is in my bag," he mutters. I go back into the bedroom on shaky legs. His bag is by the door, and I stare at it for a few moments. Crouching down, I unzip it to find a blue paper file on top of his clothes. Sliding it out, I open it and run my eyes over the piece of paper inside. The words jump out at me. Marriage certificate.

My heart pounds in my ears, making a whooshing sound. I go to the bed and sit, gripping the certificate in my hand even though the words have now gone blurry. I'm so lost in panic, I don't hear the shower turn off or Anton entering the room.

Then, I feel him watching me from the doorway, trying to gauge my reaction. "What the hell is this?" I finally manage to squeeze out.

"Our marriage certificate."

"We didn't marry," I whisper.

"We did. Alberto married us, remember?"

I shake my head back and forth. "No. No, he practiced. It wasn't real."

Anton laughs. It rings out against the otherwise silent room. "How stupid are you going to sound if you tell people that story?"

I look over my shoulder at the messy sheets. "And that was . . ." I trail off.

"That was us consummating our marriage," he confirms.

I feel sick and faint. I drop the certificate, and it floats slowly to the ground like it's mocking me. "You're lying," I mutter. "Please tell me you're lying."

"I'll ask someone to bring you some tea. It's good for shock."

"I don't want your fucking tea," I hiss, sweeping down to grab the paper before screwing it into a ball. "Why would you do that?"

"I told you, I wanted to make you mine. While we're discussing the news, I should tell you that you missed your birth control shot."

"No, I didn't," I say. "They always text me when it's due. I haven't had a text." He winces again, and it dawns on me that my text has been intercepted. Tears well in my eyes. The air feels thick, and I gasp to try and suck it into my lungs. Anton moves towards me with concern on his face, but I hold my arm up to stop him.

"I think you're having a panic attack," he says. "Let me help you."

I shake my head. "Stay the hell away from me." I drop to my knees to collect my shirt from the floor, then I clumsily pull it on before pushing to stand and heading for the door. He tries to grab my hand, but I shrug him away, too angry to find words. I head for the spare room across the landing.

Once inside, I lock the door and lean against it. I slam my hands over my mouth, trying to muffle the sound of my sobs. Tears spill down my cheeks, and as I slide down the door, they spill onto my thighs.

What the fuck have I done?

ANTON

I stand outside the locked spare room door with my forehead rested against it. I've fucked everything up so badly, but once I got talking, I felt it was best to rip the Band-Aid off in one go and tell her everything. Now, I've got to work on her forgiveness. I sigh, pushing off the door and heading downstairs.

I find Michael in my office, working away on his laptop. He glances up and smirks. "The deed is done?" I nod once then pour myself a large scotch, leaving out the ice. I take a large mouthful and wince as it burns my throat. "I'm guessing it didn't go well seeing as you're here drinking scotch like water instead of snuggling with your new wife."

I hold the glass up in his direction, letting him know he's got it in one, before knocking back the rest and setting the glass down to repour. He closes his laptop. "I hate to say I told you so, but . . ." I scowl, and he doesn't bother to finish his sentence.

The security monitors light up and catch my attention. I watch as the gates open and Tag's car drives in. "Fuck," I groan. Like the night can't possibly get any worse. When the car stops, Tag and Lucy get out, which only means one thing. Piper called her.

I head out to greet them, smiling wide and glancing at my watch. "It's one-thirty in the morning. You must've missed me."

ANTON

Lucy glares at me. "Where is she?" she demands.

Tag gently squeezes her shoulder in a placating manner, but she shrugs him off. I'll let her tone slide. I get why she's upset, so I nod back towards the house, and she marches past me.

"Did you have an argument or something?" Tag asks, yawning.

I've yet to tell him about my marriage and the guilty feeling returns. Tag's one of my closest men and I hate that I couldn't tell him my plans, but it would have caused too much drama with Lucy.

"Let's get a drink," I say, leading him inside to the living room. I pour us each a large one, handing Tag his and taking my own to stand by the window. "We're married," I say, keeping my back to him.

I hear him splutter, and when I turn to face him, he's wiping his chin. "I'm sorry, what?"

"Do you need me to repeat it, or are you just in shock?" I ask dryly.

He stands, and I square my shoulders. Tag won't hit me, it would cost him too much, but I know he wants to as he slams his glass on the table. "You ran off to Italy and married my wife's best friend?"

"Are you happy for us?"

"I thought you just needed the capos off your back?"

"Things got serious," I say on a shrug.

"It takes weeks to arrange a marriage, Anton." He picks his drink up again and takes a mouthful. "And you never mentioned it. I thought we were closer than that." He gives me a bitter stare.

"I know you don't understand, but trust me—"

"Trust you?" he spits. "You've kept me out of the loop, Anton. You think the families will believe in this marriage when I wasn't even there?"

"It's done," I say firmly. "Piper is my wife, and I'd appreciate your support."

He shakes his head sadly. "What choice do I have?"

"Tag, we're leaving," yells Lucy from the hall.

He smirks, placing his empty glass on the table. I follow him into the hall, where Lucy is waiting with Piper wrapped in her arms like a broken bird. I frown, stepping in front of them to block their path. "You're not leaving," I say, bending slightly to catch Piper's eye.

"Try and stop us, I dare you," snaps Lucy, trying to walk around me. I move again, stopping them.

"Don't forget how we got to this," I add, ignoring Lucy.

Piper looks up at me through her lashes, "I need a break," she whispers.

"You don't have to explain anything to him," Lucy snaps.

I glare at Tag, silently telling him to get his woman in check. He groans, rolling his eyes. "Luce," he mutters, "it's between them."

"Don't you dare stick up for him," she growls. "She's so upset, she can't even tell me what's wrong." I feel slight relief she hasn't told Lucy the truth.

I gently rub a thumb over Piper's cheek, and she allows it, keeping her eyes downcast. "One night," I whisper, "so you can process."

She nods once, and I step to the side so they can pass. Tag hits me on the shoulder, slightly harder than expected, and I glare at him. He smirks. "I'll see you in the gym in," he glances at his watch, "four hours. You deserve what's coming."

I roll my eyes. "We'll see about that."

I hardly sleep, catching maybe two hours before I'm up and showered. I catch up on some work in the office, and when I hear Ella come down for breakfast, I join her. She's been ignoring me since the wedding, so she doesn't look best pleased when I sit at the table.

"Where's Piper?" she asks, her voice cold.

"She spent the night at Tag and Lucy's."

Ella arches her brow. "She's sick of your arse already? It doesn't surprise me."

"Go and get ready for work. I'm leaving for the gym shortly."

"I can make my own way," she mutters.

"Now, Ella," I snap.

I'm already warmed up when Tag arrives. "Is Piper okay?" I ask.

ANTON

"No. She went to bed upset and woke angry as hell. I'd hate to be you right now," he says, smirking as he throws his gym bag down by the ring.

"Did she tell Lucy that we're married?"

Tag shakes his head. "And I'm denying all knowledge because when she finds out everything, she's going to explode."

"Do you wanna warm up?" I ask.

Tag laughs and climbs through the ropes. "I want to feel the burn in my muscles as I kick your arse, Martinez. Stop stalling and get in the ring."

Tag wasn't kidding. He wastes no time, landing hits the second I get in the ring. He's relentless, but I don't go down easy. He might be a cage fighter, but we spar most days, so I know his moves.

Forty minutes pass and my lungs feel like they're trying to escape my chest. I bend, resting my hands on my knees, and Tag slaps me hard on the back. "Are we done yet?" I ask, coughing violently.

"For now," he mutters.

"Are we okay?"

"I don't know if we're okay, but I feel slightly better." Tag wipes his face on his hand towel.

I step out of the ring and head for the office with Tag right behind me. Ella glances up, smiling when she spots him. They exchange a heated look, and I glare between the two. Ella's had a soft spot for Tag for years, and at one point, they wanted to marry, but then he met Lucy.

"How was Lucy this morning?" I ask, and Ella turns back to her work.

Tag scoffs. "Still mad at you. What I don't understand is why Piper hasn't told Lucy you're married? Shouldn't she be shouting it from the rooftops?"

Ella looks up again, this time her eyes burning into me. "He doesn't know?"

"Ella," I snap, my tone warning.

"Know what?"

"He tricked her into the marriage," she says, nodding to confirm her story.

Tag glares at me. "You did what?"

I shrug. "It sounds way worse than it is. Alberto practiced his words on us. Turns out, if you sign the register afterward, you're officially married."

ANTON

"That's not what happened, and you know it," snaps Ella. "You orchestrated the entire thing to make her think it was a practise run, but you knew the truth."

"Are you fucking kidding me?" yells Tag. "That can't be legal."

"It's legal," Ella chips in, "maybe just not moral."

I stand abruptly. "I don't have to explain myself. Tag, your job is to get Piper back to me now. I've been patient enough with her tantrum." I head for the door. "That's an order from your capo dei capi." I glance back. "And Tag, if I catch you looking at my sister again like that, I'll slit your throat and deliver it fresh to your wife."

Almost an hour later, I stand at the front door of my home, watching Tag's car drive through my gates. He steps out and places his shades over his eyes. I watch as he walks to the boot and pops it open. Reaching inside, he pulls Piper out. I stare open-mouthed, taking in the rope tying her arms behind her back and the thick silver tape covering her mouth.

She's making lots of noise, and when Tag takes her arm, she kicks him hard on the shin. He doesn't flinch but instead bends, taking her by the waist and throwing her over his shoulder.

"What the fuck are you doing?" I snap.

"Just following your orders, capo," he says coldly. He never refers to me with the respect he's supposed to. In all the time I've been the boss, he's never called me capo. "She didn't want to come quietly, boss, so I had to do it by force." He marches past me with her dangling upside down. I catch her eye as he passes and she's angry as hell.

He lowers her to her feet in the hallway as I step inside and close the door. "For Christ's sake, untie her," I order.

"She's a little wild, boss. Are you sure?"

"Tag," I hiss in warning.

He pulls out a pocketknife, and Piper glares at me. "Stay still. I wouldn't want to slip and hurt you," he tells her, smirking.

I shake my head in annoyance. "Relax. If he slips, I'll put a bullet in his head."

Tag cuts the rope and it falls away. Piper rubs her wrists and shoves Tag hard. He stumbles back a few steps, laughing at her attempt to hurt him. I catch her arm before she can attack him again and tug her to me. Her angry grunts through the gag tell me I'm the last person she wants to be near, but I turn her to face me regardless.

"Mia amata," I whisper, and she stills. I take the corner of the tape. "Take a deep breath," I instruct, and she does, then I rip the tape from her mouth. She growls angrily, her hands immediately covering the area.

"Motherfucker," she cries, spinning to Tag. "You piece of shit," she screams. "What the fuck are you playing at?"

"My boss requested I return you to him," says Tag with a shrug. "Just doing my job."

"Let's see if Lucy understands," she snaps.

I try to rub her shoulders, but she shrugs me off. "Keep your hands off me," she spits. "Don't ever touch me again."

"That's gonna be hard now we're married," I point out.

"Fuck you, Anton," she growls. "You're not my husband and you never will be." She heads for the stairs, running up them and slamming the bedroom door.

Tag laughs. "Something tells me this is going to be one of the biggest mistakes you ever made."

"She'll come around."

He laughs harder. "You reckon? Yah know, if you'd have come to me in the first place to discuss this ridiculous plan, I'd have talked you out of it. Maybe that's the reason you didn't include me. But Piper is not the sort of girl you can bend to your will."

"Don't talk like you know her better than me," I snap.

"You've spent a few weeks with her, Anton. You're no expert. If you were, you wouldn't have done this. And when Hulk finds out," he shakes his head, "you're gonna wish you'd talked to me first."

I sigh heavily. "Look, I can tell you everything, but you have to think like my underboss and not like Hulk's brother-in-law or Lucy's husband."

His expression turns serious. "It's an insult you're even saying that to me."

ANTON

"You'd better come and take a seat," I mutter, heading for my office.

Chapter Fourteen

PIPER

A loud knock on the door makes me jump. "Unlock the door, Piper, and join us for dinner." I scoff. He's acting like this is just a petty argument and I'm overreacting. How can he expect me to eat dinner with him and make polite conversation? "Do you realise I have a key for every door in this house?" he asks. "Make the right decision and come out yourself."

"I need some space. Give me some space," I yell.

"You can't stay in there forever. You'll need to come out and face this eventually."

I've been in this room for nine hours, and I don't plan on leaving while Anton is out there waiting to talk to me.

ANTON

My mobile phone lets out a shrill ring and I see it's Mae calling me. I answer, relieved to have someone to talk to. Maybe Anton will stop pestering me.

"Okay, hit me with it," she says. "Lucy told me you called her in the middle of the night."

"I would've called you, but I thought Ace and Hulk might come with you, and I didn't need the extra stress. Besides, you have enough going on."

"Don't be crazy. I'd always come if you needed me. What was so bad that you called in the middle of the night?"

"Mae, I don't know where to start. I've done something stupid, but—"

She cuts in excitedly. "You had sex with the mob boss, didn't you?"

I lose my nerve. I'm so embarrassed about the whole thing that I let her think having sex with Anton is my dilemma. "Yeah," I sigh, "and he treated me like crap after. It reminded me of Hulk."

"Oh, Pip. I'm sorry it didn't work out like you hoped. Have you spoken to him?"

"I'm embarrassed," I admit. "I can't bring myself to right now."

"When are you coming home? I miss you."

Tears well in my eyes. "I miss you too."

"I know it's exciting when you get a new man and all, but don't forget about us back here. We're your family, Piper, and we miss having you around the place."

"I'll be home soon. I promise."

We catch up on how she's feeling, and I'm happy to hear she's doing much better. Even Ace is being less overprotective of her.

We end the call promising to meet for food soon. I go into the bathroom and catch a glimpse of my pale reflection. Dark circles are forming under my eyes, and I look exhausted. "Jesus, girl, you've got to pull yourself together," I whisper, pulling the hair tie to free my bushy, unbrushed hair.

I turn on the shower and undress. I've spent hours thinking about what to do next and still I have nothing. I can't tell anyone because I feel like such a fool, and I can't stand the thought of Hulk discovering what I've done.

Stepping under the hot spray, I relax slightly. I've gone over different scenarios in my head, ones involving me and Anton making this work, but each time, I feel the same anger

ANTON

building in the pits of my stomach and realise I can't ever forgive him for this. I need advice on how to make this marriage disappear.

I step out the shower and dry quickly before heading back into the bedroom and pulling open the wardrobe. Most of my clothes were put into Anton's bedroom but some remain, and I run my hand through the new garments. Since I have a gorgeous tan from Italy and I've yet to show it off, I settle on shorts and a vest.

I unlock the door and poke my head out. Anton is nowhere to be seen, and I breathe a sigh of relief. I'm dreading having to sit and talk with him about this whole mess.

Making my way to the kitchen, I pass various security detail, all of whom nod in greeting but say nothing. In the fridge, I find some leftovers, so I pull myself up onto the countertop and cross my legs. Placing the container of food in front of me, I begin to pick out pieces of ham. It's delicious, and I groan in appreciation.

"I love the sounds you make when you eat." Anton's low rumbling voice startles me, but I ignore him and continue to pick at the leftovers. I feel him move closer and my heart slams in my chest like it's trying to break free. "I want to introduce you to so much more, just so I can watch you enjoying it." He steps into view, and I glance up. "I'll take you to the clubhouse tomorrow. You can stay there for a few days." I'm surprised, but I don't show my reaction. He smiles slightly. "I'm sure you're missing the place, and despite what you think, you're not a prisoner."

"Where will you be?" I ask, wondering if he's coming too cos that will certainly piss Hulk off.

"I have business to attend to. I won't be around much and that's not fair on you. Ella is visiting our mother."

"Suddenly you care about what's fair for me?" I ask, arching a brow and going back to picking at the leftovers.

"I know you hate me right now, Piper, but I'm hoping in time, you'll forgive me and see why I did it."

"Why did you do it?" I ask, finally looking him in the eye.

"I'm not a patient man. I see what I want, I take it. I wanted you."

"I'm not some piece of furniture you can just claim."

He smirks. "Really? That's how the biker life works, isn't it? Don't the men lay claim?"

I narrow my eyes. "That's different and you're not a biker."

"But Hulk is . . ." He trails off. "If he'd have done this, you'd allow it?"

"Hulk's hurt me a lot," I say, avoiding his gaze, "but he'd never do this to me. You should know I'm going to get some advice on how to annul this sham of a marriage."

"That won't happen," he says with confidence. "No one will annul my marriage without my say-so."

"Married or not, I'm not with you. I'm going to go about my life and pretend you don't exist. It would be much easier if you annul the marriage."

He smirks. "Go about your life and crawl back to Hulk?"

I shrug. "Maybe."

He goes silent, and I eventually look up into his stormy eyes. His fists are balled at his sides and his jaw is tight, like he's clenching his teeth. "To make me look like a fool would be a mistake, Piper," he murmurs.

"Is that a threat?" I ask.

"Yes," he replies without hesitation. "I'll kill any man who touches you . . . don't test me on that. The war with the club will be messy." He spins on his heel and leaves the room, and I stare after him. His intense glare has left me hot under the collar and I flop back on the countertop, staring up at the ceiling. How can I hate him so much, yet still lust after him like a whore? "I'm fucked," I whisper out loud. "Truly fucked."

"You okay?" Ella appears beside me, looking down with an amused expression.

"I'm so confused," I admit. "I'm giving myself a pep talk."

Ella picks some of the ham from the leftovers and pops it into her mouth. "Tell all."

"I'm listing all the reasons why I should stay away from your brother," I explain.

She nods enthusiastically. "Oh, I totally, one hundred percent, agree. He's bad news." Her tone is mocking, and I scowl playfully.

I hold a finger up in the air. "Number one, he's got heartbreaker written all over him." She nods in agreement. I add a second finger. "Number two, he tricked me into marriage. Who the hell does that?"

"Complete psycho," says Ella, shrugging.

"Number three," I add a finger, "he blackmailed me into dating him."

"Ouch, maybe that's the red flag that should have sent you running?"

I scowl again. "You're missing the part where I said blackmailed me."

"Sorry, right, go on to number four," she urges, pulling up my fourth finger.

"He's too bossy. We'd fight all the time because I hate authority."

"So true. The power of being a Mafia boss has gone to his head," she teases. "He bosses everyone around like it's his job."

"I'm his wife, not one of his staff," I point out.

Ella grins and repeats, "His wife?"

I sit up, and she steps back, laughing. "Technically," I say, shrugging. "At least I am on paper."

"All of your reasons so far are spot-on," she tells me, taking the leftovers to the table and sitting down as she continues to eat.

"What else?" I ask, letting my feet dangle over the edge of the countertop. "Give me more."

She tips her head to the side, thinking for a second. "Don't forget the nice houses he owns," waving her finger at me. "Complete rich bastard, so annoying."

I pout. "You're supposed to be helping."

She laughs. "Okay, he has a crazy mother who he sent away. He might have her genes and turn mad himself. You don't want to have to deal with that."

"Your mum is sick. Mental illness does not equal crazy," I say pointedly. "He has serious mood swings. I never know where I stand with him." I add the fifth finger.

"He owns a lot of businesses, so he'll never be home," says Ella. "You'll probably spend more time with his annoying sister than him."

"That sounds terrible," I joke.

"And he has no experience with women." She frowns. "Actually, he does. What I mean to say is he has no relationship experience, so the chances are, he'll screw it up all the time."

"There's been a lot of women?" I ask, jumping down and joining her at the table.

"Exactly. That's reason number six—he's had more women than hot dinners."

I smirk. "Explains a lot."

Ella screws her face up. "Gross."

ANTON

"What would you say to me if I was your best friend and he wasn't your brother?" I ask.

She ponders my question. "So, let's get it straight. A gorgeous rich man, with lots of power, forced you to go on numerous dates with him, paid for your hair, clothes, and makeup, also paid for dinner and Champagne . . . flew you to Italy to meet his family and friends, no expense spared, tricked you into marrying him."

"You're making it sound like a fairy-tale," I argue.

"But it's not a fairy-tale," she agrees, "and he isn't a prince here to rescue you. But," she grabs my hand, "he does appear to really like you. And don't get me wrong, I don't agree with anything he's done, but I kind of like having you around, and I think you're good for him."

I groan. "Don't side with him," I beg. "He's lied and tricked me. When I get old and my grandchildren ask me what my wedding day was like, I won't be able to share stories of drinking Champagne and having my makeup done with my bridesmaids. I'll never be able to tell this story because it's embarrassing. He made sure it was, so I couldn't tell anyone what he'd done."

"Tell him that," she says. "Tell him how you feel, and he'll fix it. He just wants you to be happy."

I shake my head. "I can't, Ella. I hate him for what he's done, and I can't forgive him. I'll find a way out of this marriage if it's the last thing I do."

I wake the following morning with a start. Anton is sitting on the bed staring down at me. I sit up quickly, moving away from him. "I locked the door," I snap, staring at the now open bedroom door.

He holds up a key. "I won't see you for a few days. I needed to say goodbye."

"Goodbye," I snap.

"Piper," he mutters, "we can't go on like this."

"I told you already, we're not staying married."

He sighs impatiently. "And I told you, we are. The sooner you accept it, the better."

I throw the sheets back and get out of bed. "How long will you be gone?"

"A few days. I'll drop you off once you're dressed." He stands to leave. "And, Piper, don't make any mistakes while you're back there."

ANTON

Michael stops the car outside the gates of the clubhouse. Scar is opening them as Piper jumps out, then she sticks her head back into the vehicle. "I don't need you to walk me inside," she says before slamming the car door.

"Pop open the boot," I tell Michael, stepping out the car and rounding the back. I grab her bag, and she snatchers it from me. Before she can march away, I grab her arm and tug her back to me. "Can I trust you?" I ask. She scoffs, and it pisses me off further. "I don't want to kill him, Piper, but I will," I warn.

"And I'll hate you even more," she mutters.

I place a finger under her chin and tip her head back to look at me. "You're angry, I get it. Don't make hasty decisions that you'll regret." I place my lips against hers. She doesn't respond, and I smile against her mouth. "Mia amata, you're testing my patience, and I love it."

A couple days have passed since I dropped Piper at the clubhouse. I've been busy the entire time, yet all that's occupied my mind is her and what she's doing. I must've picked up my mobile a thousand times to call her before talking myself out of it. She needs time to cool off. Time to miss me. Absence makes the heart grow fonder . . . or so they say.

One thing I know for sure is that Hulk is on a club run, so he isn't with my wife. It's the reason I'm sitting in a car opposite a container shipment yard. Hulk arrived here almost forty minutes ago to meet a fake buyer that I've set up.

Michael checks his watch again and sighs. "You think he's on to us?"

I shake my head. "He isn't that clever," I mutter.

Our guy finally appears, and I breathe a sigh of relief. I'm not used to doing this kind of shit. Stakeouts are for cops and men on my payroll, but I need to have all the facts before I take it further, so Ace can't tell me I'm wrong.

Axe gets into the back of the car, and Michael drives away. I turn to the back seat. "Well?"

"He wants to cut a deal. Says he can get me a good amount every week. He gave me a sample." Axe holds out a small dealer bag of cocaine, and I take it. I lick my finger and dip it in the powder before rubbing it on my gums. I nod at Michael, who is watching me out the corner of his eye. "It's our shit," I confirm. The quality is the best out here, that's how I know.

"He said I can't tell anyone or the deal is off," continues Axe. "He was really shady."

Michael shakes his head angrily. "Why do they always get fucking greedy?" It's not the first time people have tried to rip me off.

"It's human nature. It's hardly enough to make even a small dent in our empire, which confirms that he's doing this to get one over on me. It's personal. Hulk doesn't need the money."

Michael shrugs. "I'd usually say that anyone stupid enough to fuck with you must be desperate, but we know Hulk isn't. I think you're right—he wants to get one over on you. He hasn't made a secret of the fact he hates the club is in partnership with us. Maybe it's his way of rebelling?"

"Or maybe he plans to stash money away to lure my wife from me," I muse. When you get everything you want, it's hard not to believe everyone is out to take it away.

"We need to take this to Ace," Michael says. His mobile rings and he answers. After a few short words, he disconnects. "That was Piper's doctor," he tells me. "She's called him to book in for her shot."

I smirk, surprised it took her so long. "When?"

"Two days. She pushed for today, but he put her off. Also, she's taken the morning-after pill." My head whips round fast to look at him, and he winces. "Sorry. The doc wanted to make it clear it was nothing to do with him. She went to the pharmacy."

"Motherfucker," I mutter, glaring out the window.

His mobile rings again, but this time, he answers through the car handsfree. "Yep?"

"Boss, it's Conner." He pauses before adding, "We've spotted Lorenzo. I've texted you the address."

ANTON

It's the break we've been waiting for, so we can't waste a second. He's slipped through the net too many times already.

Michael turns the car around, and we head straight to the address. Conner is waiting at the end of the road. He steps to the car and bends to talk to us. "It's the house with the green door," he says, pointing. "He hasn't come out, and I think he's the only one in there. The road is pretty quiet. No one's curtain twitched to see what I'm up to, and I haven't seen anyone walking around here." I nod.

Michael drives down a side street and parks up. He gets out and goes in the boot, and when he returns, he has some police-issued bulletproof vests. Axe laughs. "I thought I'd done my job for today, and now, I'm pretending to be an officer of the law?"

"You get a chance to work alongside Anton Martinez. It doesn't happen often, and you might learn something." Michael says.

We step out the car and make our way towards the house. A man walking his dog eyes us suspiciously, and Michael smiles and flashes his fake police badge. "Evening, sir. We're conducting a search of this area for a suspected drug dealer. It would be wise to get back to your home and lock your doors. Stay clear of any windows, we don't know if this guy is armed." The man nods and rushes off, dragging his dog behind him.

We get to the house, and Axe and Connor head around the back in case he decides to make an escape. I step to the front door and try the handle. It's locked. I knock loudly and then open the letterbox. "Police! Open the door!"

As expected, he doesn't answer, but I know he can't go anywhere. "Mr. Lorenzo Corello. We're here for your protection. We have reason to suspect Anton Martinez is on his way to see you now. Councillor Smart sent us and asked us to escort you into protective custody immediately." Michael gives me a quizzical look, and I smirk and shrug my shoulders. If this doesn't work, I'll kick the door in, but I'm trying not to draw attention to us. The lock on the door clicks, and we exchange an amused look.

As soon as it's open enough for me to get my foot in the door, I shove my way inside, taking Lorenzo by surprise. He falls back against the wall, stumbling. I stand over him, giving him a pitying look. He tries to scoot away, and I laugh.

ANTON

"Pathetic." I sigh. "You're looking old, Lorenzo. Running doesn't suit you."

"Times are hard if you have to do the dirty work yourself, Anton," he hisses.

"I like to keep a hand in when it comes to cleaning up the streets. I'm passionate about tying up loose ends, and you, sir, are the last loose end in a long line of arseholes who fucked up."

Michael cuffs Lorenzo's wrists behind his back. "I'm disappointed, Michael. You're supporting the man who killed your capo in front of your very eyes," growls Lorenzo.

"Anton is my capo. He's a born leader. You said it yourself."

"You can take me out, but I already have my men in place with a plan. It's too late. They'll rise against you and The Rebellion. You'll never rest again."

"This is not an episode of *The Hunger Games*, old man. There will be no uprising. Now, shut the fuck up," snaps Michael as he hauls him to his feet. "And where are your men? Leaving you alone was careless."

I dial Hulk's number. "What?" he answers gruffly.

"Oh, I'm sorry, Hulk. Are you busy?" I ask sarcastically.

"I'm about to go see Piper," he retorts, and my fist clenches. "She seems sad, and I know just how to cheer her up." There's amusement in his voice, but I refuse to rise to his bate.

Keeping my voice calm, I say, "That'll have to wait. I have something way more important. We have Lorenzo. Tell Ace I'll save this one for him, but it needs to be done before the day is over." I disconnect the call and follow the men back to the car.

When The Rebellion finally arrive, it's dark. I open the garage door, and they follow me inside. I open the trap door and lead them into the underground tunnels.

Inside the room, it's dark and damp. If these walls could talk, they'd tell a grim tale of death and torture. I press a switch and a dim light flickers on. In the corner, tied to a wooden stool, is Lorenzo. He doesn't look so smug after his beating from me. I clench my fists when I think

ANTON

of the sound they'd made against his skin. The urge to finish what I started is strong, but Ace needs this after everything he and Mae went through.

Lorenzo smirks. "You had to bring your pussies to back you up?"

"No, I was happy to get one of my men to slit your throat. But then you went and made it all personal, and now there's a line of people who want in on your ending," I drawl, keeping my tone flat and bored.

"Can we hurry this up? We have a party to get to." We all turn at the sound of Tag's voice. I hadn't expected him to be here to see this. Watching your father die isn't something you can just wipe from your mind, and even when they deserve it, it still haunts you night after night. I should know. "Hey, Pops, you don't look so good." He grins, but I see the hurt behind those eyes. He hides it well, but he can't hide it from me. I've known him too long.

"Matteo," says Lorenzo, almost in a whisper.

Tag ignores him and looks straight to me. "You didn't think I'd want to see this?" he asks, shaking my hand.

"He's your father," I sigh, "I didn't want to put you in that position." Tag steps closer to Lorenzo. There's something different about the look in his eyes, and I can see why people fear Matteo Corallo . . . in and out of the cage.

"He tried to have me killed, and then he planned to take my wife," he spits. "I've waited a long time to see him suffer."

"It's our way of life, Matteo. It wasn't personal," his father says firmly.

"Are you serious? I'm your fucking son! It doesn't get more personal than that. I tried to help you. I lied to Conner to keep your waste of space arse alive!"

We lied to my father after Lorenzo crossed the mob. It seems so long ago now, so much has happened.

"Do it, kill me. You'll spend the rest of your days and nights remembering this moment," Lorenzo growls, pulling hard on the ropes holding him to the chair. Tag punches him. It's fast and unexpected, but Lorenzo smirks. His lip splits and crimson fluid drips down his chin. "You still hit like an untrained, feral pussy," he spits.

ANTON

"Full of encouragement," Tag scoffs. "You were always so positive," he adds, wiping his fist.

"You were nothing before I put you in that cage," Lorenzo yells.

"I was a fucking kid. You didn't want a son, you wanted a killing machine."

"And you failed at that. You're gonna let that biker piece of shit slit my throat? The Mafia affiliated with biker scum . . ." He spits on the ground angrily. "Conner would turn in his grave."

"Conner was a piece of shit, just like you. We've never been so well off. The power we have is more than you could ever have dreamed of," shouts Tag.

"Ella was always a whore. Even as a child, she'd use those big eyes to get what she wanted. Can you blame a man going there?"

I step forward, a growl leaving my throat at the callous mention of Ella's sexual abuse. Tag stops me by placing his hands to my chest. "Don't. He wants you to kill him quick. Stick to the plan."

Ace steps forward. "I told you I'd kill you," he says. "The most satisfying thing," he continues, pulling out his blade slowly, "is that now I know just how you feel about bikers, it makes it all the sweeter."

"Fuck you. Your bitch was worth it. That tight pussy begged to feel a real man."

Ace stabs the blade into Lorenzo's hand. He can't move it away because it's bound to the arm of the chair. He grits his teeth but doesn't make a sound. "I love the feel of flesh breaking," Ace murmurs, satisfaction written across his face.

"We should leave you to it," I say. "The smell is making me want to join in."

As we leave the room, the sound of Ace's exerted breaths and the slashing of flesh follow us.

I inhale fresh, clean air into my lungs as soon as we step outside. Relief floods me. We finally have the fucker. Now that he's gone, the families can relax. Michael goes inside to make some calls to the capos as Tag pats me on the shoulder. "There's a party tonight at the club. Why don't you come?"

"What's the party for?" I ask.

"Not sure. Those fuckers throw a party for anything. Look, I'd like to have a drink with you. Things have been weird lately. Now Lorenzo's gone, we should celebrate. Besides,

ANTON

your wife will be there, and if you leave her to Hulk, well..." he trails off. I glance over at Hulk, who's waiting by his bike. Tag's right. I haven't seen Piper for three days. It's time.

Chapter Fifteen

PIPER

I'd convinced myself that a party was exactly what I needed this evening. But since the guys returned, bringing Tag and Anton along with them, I feel less in the party spirit.

Mae is angry with Ace for taking Mystique along for the ride on Lorenzo's killing. And despite the fact she's ignoring him, he's got her pinned to his side, refusing to let her move anywhere without him.

Anton hasn't made a move to speak to me, and I'm not sure if that pisses me off even more. Since he dropped me here, he's not called or texted, and I should be pleased, but deep down, I'm not. That just confuses me more.

ANTON

I down another shot, miserably wondering what my life's become.

Ace climbs up on the bar. "Thanks for coming," he begins, and the chatter in the bar dies down. "You're probably all wondering why I called you here. After the last few weeks, things have been tense, and I thought we could all do with some good news." He jumps down from the bar and stands next to Mae, who looks completely baffled by his speech. "I'm not getting any younger, so I thought it was about time I took claim to a fantastic, amazing woman."

My heart beats excitedly for Mae. This is what she wanted, and I can't hide my smile as she stares at him in disbelief. There're a few cheers among The Rebellion. "Mae wasn't on my radar. We've always been friends, and she's the one I'd go to if I couldn't handle shit, so I don't know why it took me so long to see it. She's everything our kind of men need in an old lady. So," he smiles down at Mae lovingly, and my heart warms, "meet my old lady." He takes her hand and holds it up for everyone to see. The room erupts with joy, and they're embraced in hugs of congratulations.

I watch from a distance. I can't get to them just yet, so I'll wait my turn. "Aww, young love." I stiffen at the sound of Anton's voice close to my ear. "Is that how you wanted it, Piper? A big announcement and a biker party?" My gut instinct is to answer no. When I really think about it, I don't want all this fuss, but I'm not confessing that to Anton.

"Did you have a nice break?" I ask casually.

"Did you miss me?"

"No. I didn't even think about you." That's a lie. I spent almost every hour of every day either thinking about him or talking about him with my girls.

"Jesus, what the hell is she doing here?" he mutters, looking annoyed. I spot Ella talking to Hulk. She's sobbing, and Anton rushes to her, practically pushing Hulk out the way. He wraps her in his arms and leads her outside.

After a few minutes, curiosity gets the better of me, so I head out too. After all, she's my friend now. Anton is quietly talking to Ella, wiping her tears with his thumbs. "Is everything okay?" I ask.

He doesn't bother to look at me before muttering, "Fine. Go back inside." He almost sounds irritated by my presence, and I won't stay where I'm clearly not wanted.

I turn and run straight into Hulk's arms. He catches me, keeping his arms around me.

"Where's the fire?" he jokes, stroking his hands up and down my arms.

"Piper, come here," Anton demands firmly, and I roll my eyes.

"Since when did you become a lap dog for the Mafia?" Hulk whispers, smiling down at me. He's right. I've never been one to do as I'm told, so I step around Hulk and go back inside.

I'm in bed at the clubhouse, staring up at the ceiling, when my mobile flashes with a message.

Ella: Come now. He needs you.

I contemplate ignoring the message. Anton doesn't need me. He doesn't need anyone. Before I can decide what to do, she sends another.

Ella: Please, Piper. I know you're mad with him but come for me.

I groan, throwing the sheets back and getting out of bed. He doesn't deserve my help, but he's gonna get it anyway . . . for Ella.

Fifteen minutes later, I pass the driver a twenty and climb out the taxi.

I punch the security code into the keypad and wait patiently as the gate slides open. As I approach the house, I notice all the lights are on and it unsettles me. Something bad has happened. I get to the door and hesitate. Do I need to knock now I'm his wife? I reach for the handle, surmising it'll probably be locked and surprised when it opens.

I pause, taking in the scene before me. The beautiful artwork that adorned the walls is carelessly thrown across the floor, torn and broken. The large vases that used to stand proudly by the stairs are smashed to pieces, now lying amongst other debris. Ella is sitting on the bottom step, tear stains marking her cheeks, but when she sees me, she stands, wiping her face. "You came," she whispers.

ANTON

I nod, closing the door and stepping inside. "What happened?"

A loud crash comes from Anton's office, and she winces. "He's upset," she whispers. "I wasn't sure who to call."

"Why is he upset, Ella?" I ask.

She begins to cry again, her shoulders shaking. "She's dead. Mother's dead."

My eyes widen. I wasn't expecting those words to fall from her mouth. "How?" The last I heard, she was in a secure unit receiving the help she needed.

She cries harder, and I rub her back, gently shushing her. "She did it herself. Saved her medication every day until she had enough to end it."

"I'm so sorry," I whisper.

"He won't listen to any of us," she continues, nodding towards the office. "Michael suggested I call you."

I'm pretty sure I'm the last person Anton needs to see, but I head for the office anyway. The broken glass crunches under my feet, which alerts Tag and Michael. They both turn to me, and relief washes over Tag's face.

Anton is in the middle of the room with his back to us. My heart breaks for him. I've never seen such raw emotion from a man. "Anton, Piper is here," says Michael firmly.

"Get her out," he growls, his chest heaving from exertion.

"Leave us," I whisper, and Tag hesitates. "I'll be fine," I reassure him.

"Don't listen to her. I give the damn orders. Get her out of here," Anton yells.

I square my shoulders and push through Michael and Tag. "Do not speak to me like that. I'm your wife!" I snap. I hear Tag and Michael retreat from the room.

Anton eventually turns his angry face to me. "I don't want you here," he growls.

"You're not the boss of me," I say clearly, placing my hands on my hips. He pushes his face into mine, his eyes wide, but instead of anger, I see pain. I tenderly place my hand against his cheek. "I'm not leaving you like this," I reassure him.

"Do you realise how easy it would be for me to snap your neck right now? I could wipe you out just like that." He clicks his fingers. "I could

ANTON

lock you under this house, and they'd never find you."

The only way men like Anton can deal with pain is to turn it to anger, but I refuse to let him intimidate me. "I know," I whisper, nodding, "but instead of ending me, why don't we get out of here?"

"You hate me," he mutters. "Why are you here?"

I take his hand in mine, and he stares down at it. "We can ask questions later. Right now, let's forget everything else and just be us. Me and you."

Anton lets me lead him from the room. His hand loosely hangs in mine. Everyone looks up as we pass, but I don't speak. I'm scared of breaking the silence in case Anton snaps out of this daze he seems to have fallen into.

The early morning air hits us, and I feel him shiver as we continue out the gates and towards the river. It's too late for partygoers but too early for morning runners, and the silence is deafening.

We walk along the River Thames. The dark, murky water seems calm, and I'm thankful that everywhere seems peaceful. Maybe it'll help Anton get his head together.

He suddenly stops. I'm slightly ahead, so he jerks me back and then cages me against a wall. We stare at one another. "What do you need?" I whisper.

He runs his thumb over my lips. "To make it stop," he murmurs, and I see the pain in his eyes again.

I place a gentle kiss against the side of his lips. "I'm so sorry."

He closes his eyes. "How did she get away with storing her meds like that?"

"She wasn't well," I say, pulling him to me and wrapping my arms around him. "You did everything you could."

"I sent her away," he mutters into my neck. "She died hating me."

"Anton, she wasn't thinking about any of that, I'm sure. She was looking for peace."

He pulls back slightly. "How do you know?"

I frown. "I don't. But isn't that what all people want when they take their own life?"

"She wanted to be with him," he spits, pushing away from me, the anger returning. "She'd rather be with him than us, her own children."

ANTON

"But she isn't with him," I say, and he turns back to me. "He's in hell. She can't be with him there."

A strange look passes over his face before he takes a deep breath. "You're right. They're not together."

I smile, holding out my hand. "Exactly." He takes it, and we walk some more, this time in silence.

※

We return home an hour later. Anton is more relaxed, although quiet, and I'm relieved when we go inside and the place has been cleaned. Michael steps from the office. "Ella went to bed," he tells us. "Tag gave her a pill to help her sleep. Do you need anything?"

"No," snaps Anton, taking me by the hand and pulling me towards the stairs. I allow it, knowing I'll sneak out once he's asleep. We get into the bedroom, and Anton shrugs out of his clothes. He stops when he realises I'm removing nothing. "Stay," he says.

"Just until you're asleep," I tell him.

He shakes his head, rounding the bed to where I am. "No, Piper, stay . . . forever." He begins to pull at my clothing until I'm down to my underwear. "I'm sorry I fucked up so much," he adds, "and you'll never hear me apologise, but for once, I *am* sorry." He goes to his wardrobe and pulls out a soft T-shirt, walking back to me and pulling it over my head.

As I climb into bed with him, my mind is swimming in confusion. When he's like this, I want to believe we're possible, but deep down, I know he'll be moody and bossy again by sunrise. He pulls me to him, wrapping himself around me, making it impossible for me to escape once he's asleep. Maybe he guessed my plan.

ANTON

I wake with a throbbing erection. The sunlight illuminates the room, and I blink a few times to clear my blurry vision. Piper is out cold beside me, and I smile to myself. I fully expected her to run out of here the second she got a chance. Her arms are above her head and her hair is splayed across the pillow. My shirt has ridden up her body, giving me a glimpse of her pink cotton knickers. My cock strains harder, wanting to get to her.

I place a gentle kiss against her cheek, but she doesn't stir. I move down the bed and between her parted legs. Gently running my finger along the apex of her inner thigh, I hook her knickers and move them to one side. Her scent hits me and the craving to taste her gets stronger. I lean closer, and she begins to stir. I swipe my tongue along her opening, and she jolts awake, but before she can protest, I bury my mouth against her, sucking and tasting her. She looks down, her eyes full of heat, and I know she won't stop me. Seconds later, she's writhing around on the bed, gripping the sheets in her hands and panting through the pleasure.

I crawl up her body, occasionally kissing her clammy flesh. Lowering my mouth to her, she kisses me, raking her nails down my back and wrapping her legs around my waist. I reach between us, lining myself up at her entrance, and she uses her legs to pull me closer, impatiently waiting for me to enter her.

I rest my hands either side of her head and slowly ease myself in. She's tight, and I groan as her pussy clamps around my cock. I feel my control slipping with each thrust, she feels so good. She takes my hand, guiding it to her throat. I wrap it around, applying enough pressure to hear her gasp for breath as I begin to move faster, my movements jerky as I climb higher. She begins to tremble beneath me, clawing at my shoulders and back, whimpering with pleasure. It sends me over with her and we climax together, panting desperately until wetness creeps between us and our bodies are damp with perspiration. I fall down beside her and stare up at the ceiling. "Cancel your doctor's appointment today," I tell her, and I feel her eyes on me. "Everyone's on my payroll, Piper, don't forget that."

I get up and make my way to the shower. Minutes later, I'm under the spray, replaying the way her body reacted to me, when she appears, leaning against the door frame and watching me.

"Why can't you be conventional?" she asks.

"Conventional?" I repeat, rubbing soap into my chest and watching her.

She shrugs. "If you liked me, why didn't you ask me on a date—"

"I did," I cut in.

ANTON

She rolls her eyes. "Without blackmailing me," she adds. "Dates, spending time together, eventually asking me to marry you. That's how things work. That's how it should have happened."

"According to who?" I ask, rubbing shampoo into my hair.

"To every normal person in this world," she says, exasperated. "It's just how it works."

"Piper, I murder people. I sell drugs. I once slit the throat of a man while his six-year-old daughter hid in the wardrobe, and that's not the worst thing I've done. My love, there is nothing conventional about me, but that's why you're drawn to me, right?"

"Not true. I had no choice in any of this."

I turn off the shower and step out. Her eyes scan my body, and I grab a towel to cover up. "You had a choice," I tell her. "Even Tag told me you hate to be backed into a corner. It's no secret you're a strong, feisty woman. Hell, that's half the reason I liked you. You could have stood up to me at any time, but you didn't." I kiss her cheek as I pass, heading for the wardrobe, and she follows.

"You threatened to show a video of me stripping to my family, to my dad."

"And, most importantly, to Hulk," I say, arching a brow. I take out a leather belt, and she eyes it, biting her lip. "So you got your tits out on stage," I say with a shrug, "you were drunk, and your parents would've forgiven you. You know what I think?" I ask, holding the belt tight in my hands. She shakes her head, and as I step closer, she backs up until she hits the wall. Her eyes follow the belt as I lift it, pressing it to her throat. Her nipples immediately harden and heat fills her eyes. "I think you wanted me to take control because your life was spiralling." I place more pressure. "I think," I move my lips to hers until they're almost touching, "you'd hit rock bottom and that's why you were in my bar, drunk on shots and dancing on my stage."

I tilt my head, kissing along her jaw, and she closes her eyes, her lips parting slightly. I press the belt harder, and her eyes shoot open as I push my erection to her opening. She automatically opens her legs, allowing me to sink in. I drop the belt and lift her until her legs wrap around my waist. "He broke you, and I'm going to be the man who fixes you." I slam my mouth over hers, kissing her until she's moaning in pleasure.

I leave Piper to rest after our wardrobe encounter. She was weak as I carried her back to bed, and she didn't protest when I covered her over and kissed her on the forehead, telling her to sleep.

Downstairs, Ella is in the kitchen staring into a cup of coffee. She looks up at me with tears in her eyes. "How are you?" she asks before shaking her head and giving an empty laugh. "That's a stupid question."

I rub my hand over her cheek, forcing her to look at me. "We'll be fine. Me and you against the world."

"And Piper?" she asks.

I nod. "And Piper."

"Is she staying?"

"Yes. I'll take her to get some things from the clubhouse later today. I want her to tell her parents about the marriage."

"Do you think they'll be okay?"

I shrug, pouring myself a coffee. "What choice do they have? It's done."

"Maybe you could take her shopping," suggests Ella.

"Shopping?" I repeat.

"She hates the things in the wardrobe. They're not her style."

I sit down. "She never said."

"She's too polite. Take her shopping, so she can choose her own things to wear."

An hour later, Piper knocks on my office door. I'm relieved she didn't enter two minutes earlier when I was cancelling her doctor's appointment to get her shot. "Feel like shopping?" I ask, and she shrugs. "Ella said you don't like the clothes I got you."

"I didn't know if they were just mine or clothes you kept for passing women," she says with a small smile.

I laugh. "We'll get you some clothes on the way to the clubhouse."

"The clubhouse?" she asks, looking hopeful.

ANTON

"To get your things," I say, picking up my mobile phone and wallet.

"Why?" she asks.

"We can't be married and live separately," I tell her, grabbing my jacket.

"Anton," she begins, but I shake my head.

"Not again, Piper. Let's not ruin the day with your protests."

"I just think it's a bit soon," she continues as I pass her. "Maybe we can take it slower."

"Slower than marriage?" I ask, laughing. "Shoes," I tell her, waiting by the door.

She slips her feet into trainers. "You're being too pushy."

"I know what you're trying to do," I say, opening the door and ushering her out. "You're putting off telling your parents."

"They'll be so upset," she admits.

Michael opens the car door, and I wait for Piper to slide in before following her. "They have to be told eventually."

"But we've been dating for such a short time. Can't we wait a while longer?"

"No."

"And then there's Hulk," she says, wincing when I glare in her direction. "He'll lose his mind."

"Do you think I care what that piece of shit thinks?" I snap.

She folds her arms over her chest and stares out the window. "I don't want you to fight."

"This ends today with him knowing everything and you walking away with me. If that means I go to war with the club, then so be it."

"You don't mean that," she hisses. "I'm not worth it."

I grin, taking a handful of her hair and tugging her head back until we're eye to eye. "You think my troubles with Hulk are solely over you?" I scoff. "I'm a businessman, a good one, and I have my own score to settle with Hulk. It has nothing to do with you."

Michael parks in a no park zone on a road where there are several nice stores that cater to the kind of clothes I want Piper to choose. He waits by the car as we're flanked by three bodyguards. "Is this really necessary?" asks Piper, glancing at the huge men. I ignore her and open the door to the first shop.

ANTON

We're met by the owner, who is the sister of one of my associates. "Mr. Martinez," she greets, smiling but looking genuinely terrified that I'm standing in her shop.

"Go find clothes," I say to Piper, and then I pull out my mobile and check my emails. Piper doesn't move. Instead, I feel her eyes burning into me. "What?" I ask.

"I don't wear these kinds of clothes," she hisses. "No offence," she adds to the shop owner.

"Piper, why is everything so damn difficult with you? Get eveningwear for events. I had the wardrobes at all my properties fully stocked, yet you don't seem to wear anything from them."

"Because I didn't buy them. You did."

I glare at her impatiently. "Which is why I'm standing in a shop asking you to choose some fucking clothes."

She rolls her eyes and stomps off to look through the rails of clothing. After thirty minutes of looking, Piper chooses eveningwear, daywear, and some loungewear. She refuses point blank when I suggest underwear.

Next, we head to the clubhouse. As we roll to a stop outside, I take Piper by the arm. "Before we go in there, there're some ground rules. If you want to keep this from your parents a while longer, fine. Grab whatever you need, then we'll leave. The quicker, the better, because quite honestly, I don't need Hulk's bullshit today." She nods. "But, Piper, this can't go on forever. You have to tell everyone, and soon."

Chapter Sixteen

PIPER

I follow Anton towards the club entrance, and he glances back. "Why are you bringing the shopping bags?" he asks.

I shrug. "I want to show my mum." Actually, the truth is that most of this stuff is for Mae. She never goes shopping, and as Anton pointed out, the wardrobes at his house are full to bursting with new clothes. Apart from a couple evening dresses left in the car, I shopped with Mae in mind.

Stepping through the door first, I'm faced with Hulk and Ace chatting at the bar. They both turn my way, and for a second, Hulk looks pleased to see me, but then Anton steps behind me and his expression changes. He turns his back to me and my heart sinks slightly.

"Been shopping?" asks Ace.

"This woman is a shopaholic," Anton groans like it's such a hardship.

"You letting the Mafia buy your shit?" snaps Hulk. I get that familiar pain in my chest, the one I'm so used to feeling when I have any interaction with Hulk. I used to pray he'd look at me with love and treat me like his ol' lady, but these days, I'd just be happy with a smile or a less aggressive attitude.

"I can treat my woman to whatever she likes," says Anton with a smirk. "Maybe you should have done this, then she wouldn't have gotten tired of your arse."

"I wasn't talking to you," Hulk says and suddenly stands.

I sigh, taking the opportunity to quietly tell Anton, "Let's go to my room." Then I breeze past Hulk, ignoring him. I'm becoming an expert at handling his tantrums.

"You need to stop ignoring me, Piper," growls Hulk angrily. He waits a beat before adding, "Or I'll tell him everything." I stop in my tracks and spin to face him. Our eyes lock and we're in a silent standoff.

"Piper," Anton says, "what the hell's he talking about?"

My mouth opens, but words fail me. "Erm . . . nothing. He's . . . let's just go." I try to grab Anton's hand, but he pulls it away.

"Not so cocky now," mutters Hulk, turning his back to us again and sipping his drink. The urge to beat him round the head is strong. He never fails to humiliate me.

"If you have something to tell me, just say it," snaps Anton.

"She's your woman, she should tell you," he replies.

"Do you know what? It doesn't even matter, Hulk, because whatever it is, it's not going to pull us apart." Anton now grabs my hand and begins to lead me towards the stairs. My heart hammers hard in my chest.

"Is that right?" asks Hulk, and I briefly close my eyes. *Why won't he just stop?* "Because you're solid, right?" I hear the smirk in his voice.

"Keep walking," Anton hisses in a low voice so only I can hear. "When we get upstairs, you better start talking."

"So solid, she came running back to me just last week."

Anton stops, drops my hand, and slowly turns to face me, arching a brow. "Is that right, Piper?" he almost whispers, his voice low and menacing.

I feel my face burning with embarrassment. "It wasn't like that," I mutter.

His hand slides along my cheek, but it doesn't feel warm and endearing as he lifts my head to make eye contact and pinches my chin between his thumb and finger. "How was it, exactly?"

"She'll always come back, Anton," says Hulk with a grin. "But you knew that when you began chasing her just to piss me the fuck off."

Anton releases me, breaking eye contact and pasting a smirk on his face. "You think that's why I started seeing her?"

Hulk takes another sip of his drink, keeping his back to us. "We all know you're using her."

"Thanks," I snap, "because he can't possibly actually like me?"

"You missed out, Hulk. Get over it," Anton drawls.

ANTON

Ace stands. "Let's just cool things down a notch. There's no need to be arguing over women."

"You're right," says Anton, nodding, "especially when I've already won."

Hulk slams his glass down, and I groan. "You've won shit when she's still crawling into my bed."

"I didn't," I argue.

"It won't be happening again," says Anton firmly.

Hulk laughs. "You reckon? What do you say to that, Piper? Do you think you can stop turning up at my door?" I hate his cocky grin, and then I loathe myself even more knowing I'm the reason he's so full of it. I feed that ego. "Maybe this made me realise a few things," he adds. "Maybe I'm not ready to give up on us."

I stare open-mouthed. "You don't mean that, you're just saying it."

"I mean it," says Hulk. "Pick me, Piper. Not him. I'll make you my ol' lady." I inhale sharply. I've dreamed to hear those words leave Hulk's mouth, yet right now, in this moment, I feel empty. His words are too late and are meaningless when he's backed into a corner.

Anton scoffs, rolling his eyes. "Tell him why you won't be lowering yourself to be with him again, Piper," he orders, glancing my way.

I bite my lower lip. *How do I get myself into these situations?* "Anton, please," I whisper.

"Now," he snaps.

"Anton," I mumble, "please don't, not like this."

"Please don't what?" he smirks, looking cruel. "This is the moment you've been waiting for, isn't it?" I don't like the hatred in his eyes. Right now, he's every bit the mob boss that people talk about. "So, put him out of his misery and tell him why you won't be his old lady."

I begin to cry, but it's silent tears that roll down my cheeks. I want the earth to open up and swallow me whole right now. I can't tell him the truth even though he deserves to be hurt for everything he ever put me through. For every woman he slept with right after being with me. For every knockback or cruel remark. But it's not in me to do this in front of Anton. "Tell him!" Anton yells, making me jump with fright.

Ace stands, placing himself between the three of us. "We all need to calm down," he says.

ANTON

Anton shakes his shoulders out, ridding himself of the tension that was written all over his face. "You're right, Ace. Sorry." He takes a deep calming breath and then smiles at Hulk, and I brace myself for the blow that I know is coming. "We're married, Hulk. You're too late."

Everything just stops, including my breathing. It's the calm before the storm because then, without warning, Hulk pulls out his gun and points it at Anton. His face is red, angry, and full of pain. Ace yells at Hulk to put the gun down, and Anton just laughs. He actually laughs, like this whole situation isn't ripping me and the people I love apart.

"Tell me the truth, Piper," yells Hulk. The gun shakes in his hand, and I keep my eye trained on it.

Anton's bodyguards must sense the danger because they burst in, also drawing their weapons when they see Hulk. Anton casually sticks his hands in his pockets. "Piper, we're waiting," he drawls, and I want to smash his face into the wall for taking pleasure in this horrible situation.

"Hulk, please, put that away," I whisper desperately. I gently place my hand on his arm, but he shrugs me off violently and shoves me away from him. I stumble, and as Anton catches me in one arm, he draws his gun with the other.

"Don't fucking touch her again," he warns. I notice his hand is steady. He really isn't phased by any of this.

Ace stands directly in front of Hulk and stares into his face. "Son, put the gun away. She's just a woman. There're enough of them in and out of your bed for you to walk away and recover from this." Hulk's eyes fix on Ace, and I see him start to lower the gun. I breathe a sigh of relief and sag against Anton.

"Is now a good time to tell you about your kid that she aborted?" Anton asks casually. I cry out and try to get out of his strong grip. He doesn't let go, pinning me against his hard body as it shakes with laughter. "And guess who paid for the abortion."

"Motherfucker!" Ace yells as Hulk raises the gun again and shoves him away. He moves so fast that I flinch, and then the gun is at Anton's temple.

The bodyguards move towards Hulk, but Anton orders them to stand down, and I wonder

ANTON

if he's lost his mind. Hulk could pull the trigger and blow his brains out at any second.

Hulk brings his eyes to me. "Piper," he murmurs, and I hear the pain this time as his voice cracks, "tell me he's lying."

Tears roll down my cheeks. "I'm so sorry," I whisper.

He growls, taking a step back and lowering his gun. He turns his back to us, and I see his chest rise and fall like he's trying to regain his control. "Get out," he mutters.

"Hulk, I—"

"Get the fuck out of this club. You're not welcome here. Either of you," he yells.

I look to Ace for help, but he stares at me hard. "As President of this club, I back my VP on this. Get out."

"Sorry, old timer, but that's not your call," says Anton, tucking his gun away. "Not when your Vice President has been skimming money and drugs from me."

Hulk laughs and shakes his head. "Fuck you. Mafia piece of shit."

Ace stares at Hulk and then looks back to Anton. "He wouldn't do that."

"Do you think I say this shit without proof? You'll be at my office this evening at ten. We'll discuss a new deal." Anton takes my hand and pulls me from the clubhouse. I can't see from the tears and I stumble a few times. He passes the shopping bags to one of the bodyguards and then swoops me into his arms. I stare over his shoulder as we leave my home, and my heart breaks all over again.

The drive back to Anton's is a blur. I hear him say my name several times, but I can't bring myself to speak. My throat is dry and my head is pounding. All I can see is Hulk as his eyes filled with pure hatred.

The car draws to a stop outside and I open my door before Michael can and get out. I move quickly, not really thinking about the direction as I round the back of the house. "Wait," orders Anton. I march faster, desperate to put some space between us. "Piper," he yells.

"Fuck you!" I scream, breaking out into a run. "Fuck you." I keep running until I'm swept off my feet and pulled hard against Anton's chest. I try to break free, squirming and lashing out. I yell and scream and curse over and over until I exhaust myself and fall limp in his arms. He buries his face into my hair and whispers apologies until I'm completely still.

"I love you," he mutters.

"If you loved me, you wouldn't have done that," I whisper, my voice hoarse from my yelling. "You put your need to slay Hulk above me."

"I can't stand the thought of him coming between us, Piper. What the fuck was he talking about with you going to him?"

"Nothing happened," I yell. "I haven't been near him like that in a long time."

"You didn't rush to set the record straight, I felt like a fool. And then he practically confessed his undying love to you, and you just stared like a goddamn fish."

"I was in shock. He's never put himself out like that."

"Did you consider it? His offer?"

"No, of course not," I snap. "I was trying to find the right words to let him down gently, and then you waded in with your big mouth full of secrets."

"It should've been an instant reaction for you to have picked me," he spits.

"Stop telling me how to act," I scream. "I have a heart, and I'm not like you. I can't hurt people on a whim. When he asked me to choose, I realised I didn't feel anything for him anymore," I yell, waving my arms around like a crazy person.

"You didn't feel what?" he asks.

"Love," I snap, scrubbing my hands over my face. "I realised I didn't love him."

"Because you love me?" asks Anton, looking hopeful.

I release a scream, staring up at the sky. "I don't know," I yell, "because I can't think straight when I'm around you. You intoxicate my sense until all I see is you and it clouds my mind. You need to just . . ." I inhale sharply. "Stop. Just stop."

ANTON

I tap my fingers on my polished wooden desk. Ace should arrive any minute, but my mind is full of Piper. As soon as we got into the house, she ran off to the spare room and refused to come out for dinner.

Michael watches my fingers. "Do you want me to deal with The Rebellion?" he asks. I shake my head, and he sighs. "It's just you seem a little preoccupied."

"I'm fine," I mutter and take a sip of bourbon. "Am I an obsessive person?"

Michael thinks the question over for a minute before sitting up straighter in his chair. He's about to level with me, and I brace myself. "The way you've moved things along with Piper is a little out of character for you," he says cautiously. "How would you react if she wanted to leave?"

I clench my jaw, feeling tense. "She won't be leaving me."

He arches a brow. "Then maybe a little obsessed, yes."

We see Ace arrive on the security cameras and shelve our conversation. A bodyguard brings him to the office, and I'm surprised Scar is by his side rather than his son. "Take a seat," I say, pointing to the chairs set out before my desk.

Michael gets them each a drink and takes a seat off to the side of us. I lay out some photographs of Hulk packing his saddlebags with my money. Then I add pictures of Hulk with some of my product. "That proves shit," says Scar, leaning over to stare at the photographs.

I press play on the recording device that my guy wore when Hulk offered him a deal. I see the realisation dawn on Ace's face. He closes his eyes briefly and grits his teeth. "How long has this been going on?" he asks. "Why didn't you come to me straight away?"

"I needed proof. I knew you wouldn't take my word for it otherwise."

"So, what do you want from us now?" asks Scar.

"Nothing. I have Piper. You kicked her out of the club, so I got what I wanted, but there will be repercussions for what Hulk's done."

"What kind of repercussions?" asks Ace.

"The kind that will hit your finances," I say. "The kind that will cause you some problems."

"Spit it out," snaps Scar. "We don't have all night."

"I'm limiting your usage of my ports. I want to see everything you bring in. Every crate will

ANTON

be checked over by my men, and I'll take a cut of the profits."

"No way," growls Ace. "The deal was we get in whatever we need if we unload your shipments. I'm not risking my men if I'm not getting anything out of it."

"I don't need your men any longer. Thanks to the training your men provided, my men will be unloading the docks from now on. They'll be unloading your shipments, and I'll be taking a forty percent cut."

"Are you shitting me!" yells Ace, standing.

"One of your men has been screwing me over for months. You're lucky I haven't put a bullet in him. Stealing is one thing, but betrayal is worse. We made a deal. We agreed on a mutually beneficial deal and your own son fucked it up. If it wasn't for Tag, I'd have hung your boy from the London docks myself and gutted him like a fish. There's no deal here. I'm being generous even offering to work with you after this. Until I trust you, this is the only offer you will get."

"This is bullshit," Scar mutters. "We can't afford to agree to this."

I slam my hands down on the desk and glare at him. "Didn't you hear me? This is the only deal I'm offering. You turn it down and all ties between the mob and The Rebellion end tonight. None of your shipments will enter London. I'll make sure of it."

"And where the hell would you get your guns and weapons if not through The Rebellion?" growls Ace.

"You think you're the only people who bring that shit in? I have contacts all over the world. My dealings with you came around because of Tag and Lucy marrying. I can end our agreement right now and have a new shipment of goods by the morning. I'll lose no sleep over cutting our ties."

"You married into the club, Anton. You're tied through Piper now," Ace reminds me.

I laugh. "The same Piper you just kicked out of the club? You made it clear whose side you're on."

"She's Rebellion blood. No matter what, she'll always be a part of the club. Things said in anger can be resolved," says Ace.

"But not forgotten or forgiven," I reply. "The only Rebellions Piper will see from now on will

ANTON

be her parents. I'll let you break that news to Mae." I smile.

"And Piper's okay with that, is she?" asks Scar.

"Piper is my concern now, not yours. My wife, my rules. It's late, gentlemen. Michael will show you out."

I leave the office and go to the library. A few minutes later, Michael joins me. "You think they'll take the deal?" he asks.

"They don't have a choice. They won't get the goods in without it. Travelling out to other areas to get them is too risky. They need my protection and my contacts. It was a generous deal."

"I told Ace to let us know his decision by noon tomorrow."

The door opens and a bodyguard comes in looking panicked. "Boss, the girls have gone out alone. Were they supposed to?" he asks.

"What are you talking about?" snaps Michael marching for the stairs. I follow, and so does the guard. "Of course, they're not. It's late."

"They took the Bugatti too," he adds.

I whizz around to look at him and he stumbles to a stop. "They took the fucking Bugatti?" I yell, and he nods. "They'll kill themselves. Ella's driving is atrocious. How the fuck did they get out without someone seeing?"

"We didn't realise they weren't allowed out, boss. By the time we'd asked one another, they were gone."

I take deep breaths to calm myself. "You all better go and look for them. I want them found." I pull out my mobile and check the tracker app. It shows them both as being home. I groan. "They've left their phones here."

"I'll get onto the chief superintendent. He'll have a patrol car pick them up in no time," says Michael.

Chapter Seventeen

PIPER

"Are you sure about this?" Ella asks, glancing at the rundown bar.

I nod. "The guys always come here when they need headspace. Hulk will want to be away from Ace after everything that's gone down tonight."

"It looks like a pretty rough place to hide out. Maybe we should've bought a bodyguard."

"I'll be ten minutes. I just need him to hear me out."

Ella caught me sneaking out the house and offered to drive me. Turns out she quite likes adventure despite her hiding away from the world for the last few months.

I open the door to the bar and am immediately hit with the smell of beer and smoke. Despite smoking being banned in all UK public places, this bar is the kind that breaks the rules. I glance around and my eyes fall on Hulk. He's leaning against the bar, and a female is kissing her way up his neck. The bar owner, Tony, smiles when he sees me. He's used to me coming here to track down club members, especially Hulk.

Ella takes a seat at the bar, and Tony gets her a drink. I tap the female on the shoulder and politely ask her to get lost. "What the fuck are you doing here?" growls Hulk. His eyes are filled with hate, and I recoil slightly.

"I had to explain," I begin. Hulk grabs my upper arm and shoves me towards the exit. Ella stands with a look of panic on her face, but I hold up my free hand.

"I'm okay. Stay here. Tony, look after her," I order.

Hulk pushes me out into the street and releases my arm. "Don't come in here again," he yells, pointing his finger in my face. "I can't even look at you right now. You make me sick."

"I'll keep coming back until you listen to me, Hulk."

ANTON

"I don't want to listen to your bullshit excuses, Piper. If you keep following me, I'll do something I'll regret. Don't push me on this." He goes back inside, and despite his warning, I follow.

"You weren't ready for a baby and all of responsibility that came with that," I tell his retreating form.

Hulk spins back around and pushes his face close to mine. "You didn't give me a chance to decide that."

"I asked if you ever wanted kids. Do you remember that? You said no. You said you didn't want that kind of life. How could I tell you after that? I felt like I was trapping you," I say, desperate for him to understand.

"I wouldn't have said any of that if you'd have told me. I would've given it a go. I would've stepped up," he hisses.

"And you would've hated me for forcing you to live a life that you didn't want, Hulk. I've loved you for so long, and I've spent years letting you come and go from my life. I couldn't do that to a kid. You'd have gotten bored. You'd eventually have cheated on me. I had to make the right decision for both of us."

"You're wrong. I would've done the right thing. You shouldn't have made that decision without me. I may have fucked up over and over, but one thing I always knew," he pauses and presses his lips together in a hard line, "was that we would have married one day. We were always going to be together when the time was right."

"Always on your terms," I mutter. "Everything is always on your terms and when you're ready. Well, guess what, I got sick of waiting. Sick of trying. Sick of being the second choice. I deserve better."

"And you think he'll treat you better because he buys you clothes or flies you to romantic hotspots?" He shakes his head, giving a cold, empty laugh. "He's no better than me, Piper. Ask him about Italy, about Aurora."

"Hulk," hisses Ella, "shut the hell up."

"Sorry, babe. I can't keep our pillow secrets after the shit I've heard today. You forgot to tell me this one, didn't you?" he snaps, glaring at her accusingly. I stare back and forth between them, shocked.

"You're sleeping together?" I whisper.

ANTON

"It's not like that," says Ella desperately. "I was gonna tell you."

"And Aurora?" I ask. She lowers her eyes to the ground.

"So, you can sit all high and mighty, but deep down, he's the same as me. He'll fill you with kids and fuck around with other women. The only difference is . . . I've always been upfront and honest with you. I told you we weren't exclusive. But Anton, he'll make you feel like the only woman in his world, then he'll do everything behind your back. It'll hurt so much more."

I sigh, rubbing my hands over my face and feeling like I've aged ten years in the last few hours. "Earlier, you confessed to loving me, yet all along you're sleeping with Ella," I mutter. "Was that to hurt me or Anton?"

He laughs. "Don't flatter yourself."

"I'm so tired of the games and the lies and—"

"Lies," he snaps. "You're one to lecture on lies. Did you abort my kid to punish me for not loving you enough?"

I groan. "No, how could you even say that? I did it to set us both free of one another."

"And you went to him to get help?"

"What does it matter? I didn't do any of this to hurt you, Hulk, but lord knows you deserve it. You've spent years pushing me away, only to pull me back in when it suited you. You tell me you love me, then sleep with the next woman you meet. You're not ready for kids or to settle down. And I've moved on. I'm sorry I've hurt you, but it wasn't intentional. That's all I came to say."

I turn on my heel and leave, with Ella right behind me. "You slept with Hulk?" I ask accusingly once we're outside, and she looks guilty. I'm surprised how much it doesn't bother me. A few weeks ago, it would have broken my heart. "Christ, your brother will explode."

She looks past me and gulps. "Oh, crap, we have a problem."

"I wonder what brings you to this backstreet hole?" asks Anton.

I turn slowly and square my shoulders, ready for the fight I know is coming. I won't act like I've done anything wrong. Not after everything he's done to me. "What happened in Italy with Aurora?" I ask. Anton's eyes go to Ella for a second and then back to me.

"Did you meet up with Hulk?"

ANTON

"Yes," I say, and he clenches his jaw. "Aurora?" I ask again.

"Ella, get in the Bugatti with Michael," he snaps. Ella does as he says, gently squeezing my hand as she passes. Anton points to the waiting Mercedes. "Let's go."

"Did you cheat on me?" I ask, folding my arms across my chest.

"Is it cheating if you're not actually together?" he muses.

"If I had sex with Hulk since we started this whole lie, is that cheating?" I ask, tipping my head to one side and arching a brow.

A flash of anger flickers through his eyes. "I'm warning you, Piper, get in the damn car."

"I'm trying to establish the rules of our marriage," I say. "So, let me ask again, did you cheat with Aurora?"

"I had sex with her, yes."

I'm surprised by the hurt his words cause me. "Before or after you forced me into a marriage?"

"Before," he snaps impatiently.

I shake my head angrily. "Fucking men and their inability to stay faithful, even in a fake relationship," I mutter out loud. "I am so tired of men walking all over me," I add. "Fuck you, Anton."

I turn and walk in the opposite direction. "Piper," he snaps, "where the hell are you going?" I blink fast to chase the tears away. I should be relieved—it gives me a reason to walk away. "Piper, if you don't get in the car, I'll put you in it," he warns me.

I look back over my shoulder at him. "I'll scream the street down if you touch me."

"It won't make a difference. No one will help you, and screamers go in the boot." I hear his footsteps coming up behind me, and I'm about to break out into a run when a police car turns down the street towards us. I step out in the road, waving my arms, and he slams on his brakes. "Piper," says Anton in a warning tone.

The officer gets out the driver's side, and a female officer steps from the passenger side. "Please, can you help me?" I pant. "I want to get away from him and he won't let me. He threatened to put me in the boot of his car."

The male officer nods in greeting at Anton, but the female steps around the car and comes to me. "Let's get you in the car and you can tell us what happened," she says kindly.

ANTON

"Actually, Kay, I think we can leave Mr. Martinez to deal with this," her partner says.

She stares at him in confusion. "No. This lady is clearly distressed. I won't leave her here."

"Piper, think very carefully before you get in that car," Anton warns.

"Sir, please don't make threats. I'll arrest you if you continue," warns the female officer.

The male officer gives a nervous laugh. "We won't be arresting you, Mr. Martinez. I'm so sorry about this. She's new."

"It's fine," Anton sighs. "Take my wife. Let her cool off. She can't go anywhere with no money or any of her things. I'll collect her from the station in the morning," he says, keeping his eyes on me.

Once we're in the car, the female officer turns to me. "Are you okay?" she asks.

I nod. "My husband knows officers at the top, powerful people. Please don't take me to the station. If you could drop me off near the train station, that would help me so much."

"Of course," she nods, "wherever you want to go. We have a fund for victims of domestic abuse. I can access that in a few hours. I'll need some details, and you'll need to make a formal complaint against your husband, but I'll be with you every step of the way."

I spot the male officer heading back to the car. "I don't have time for that. Your colleague will take me to the station and Anton will come for me."

I watch Anton's car pass us as he drives away. He stares at me and I shiver at the coldness in his eyes. The officer gets into the car. "Can I speak with you alone, please?" I say to the female officer. "Outside?" I need her to open this door for me because it automatically locks. She gets back out and opens the door. "Thanks," I say. "I can take it from here."

"Are you sure?" she asks. I nod and go back towards the bar. Hulk is my only hope right now.

"Not you again," he growls, pushing the female from his lap.

"I need your help," I say. "I need money."

He laughs, throwing his head back. "Like I'm going to help you after what you did."

"You stole money from the mob. I need it." He laughs harder. "Get out of here, Piper."

"I need it to get me away from Anton. I know you'll jump at the chance to get back at him." It's enough to get Hulk's attention. "But right now, you need to get me out of here because Anton will be back any minute." The officer would have updated Anton on my situation, and I have no doubt he'll turn his car back around. "Is there a back door to get out of here?"

ANTON

"What do you mean, she got out of the car? And went where exactly?" I bark into my mobile phone.

"Back into the bar," explains the officer.

"Then get back in there and hold her 'til I come back," I yell, hitting my hand on the steering wheel. *What the hell is she up to?*

I reach the bar in five minutes, and the officer is standing outside looking pissed. "Sorry, she's gone."

I hold in the rage that burns through me. "Any ideas?" I ask through gritted teeth. He shakes his head, and I burst through the doors of the bar. I glare at the owner. "You have seconds to tell me where the fuck that biker piece of shit took my wife before I burn this place to the ground."

He holds his hands up in the air. "I don't know, I swear. I turned to serve a customer and they were both gone. They didn't leave out the front. The back leads onto an alley, which eventually leads to the main road."

"You hear anything, you call me." I stomp from the bar and head back to the car, then I call Michael. "She's gone. Hulk is with her."

"Shit," he mutters. "So, what now?"

"Put a call out. I want them found. I want him hanging from the bridge before sunrise. I'm heading to The Rebellion now. Meet me there." I disconnect and head straight for the clubhouse. I've never experienced the panic I have in my chest right now. I know Hulk has money. He could take her anywhere so they could start again together. My knuckles turn white as I grip the steering wheel harder.

I get to the clubhouse and the gates barely open before I drive through them at speed. The bikers standing outside having a smoke all look in my direction.

Ace steps out from amongst them and meets me as I get out the car. "It's late. What are you doing here?"

"Where is he?" I growl, hardly able to contain my anger. Michael's car screeches to a halt beside mine, and he steps out and joins me.

ANTON

"You said we had until noon tomorrow to make our decision," hisses Ace, squaring his shoulders.

"The deal is off the table," I say with as much venom in my tone as I can muster. "I want my wife to return to me before sunrise or I'll start tearing through this club." Ace looks to Michael for an explanation, but he remains silent.

Tag appears over Ace's shoulder, and his smile fades quickly when he senses the heat between us all. "What's going on?"

"Hulk has Piper," I grit out. "I need her back."

"Man, Hulk isn't here. We haven't seen him since this morning," says Tag. He steps up beside Ace and it narks me. He's supposed to be my family, yet he's standing shoulder to shoulder with the club President.

"There's a war coming brother. You need to decide whose side you're on. If Piper isn't back with me by sunrise, things will get ugly."

Tag looks uncomfortable. "I know it's hard, boss, but be patient. Piper will cool off and come home. It isn't Ace's fault that you two argued. Causing a war isn't the answer."

Lucy breezes over, and Tag sees the glint in my eye. Before he can reach her, I snatch her towards me and grip her tight around the waist. She lets out a scream, causing Ace to draw his gun and aim it towards me. "Well, let's see, *brother*," I spit out. "My wife for yours?" I back away from him.

"Shit, Anton, don't do this." Tag follows me, a pleading look in his eyes. Lucy hits my arms over and over, but I don't feel it.

"Make a choice Ace. Your son or your daughter?" I force Lucy into the car. "Stay there or I'll put a bullet in Ace," I warn, slamming the car door and locking it. Tag places his hand on the window. He won't take her back by force. The consequences for him would be too much.

"It hurts, doesn't it?" Tag sighs. "Love?"

"Not now, Tag. Call your brother-in-law and find out what the fuck he's doing."

"Your father used to tell us when we were growing up that love would ruin us. It would blind us and cause us to make stupid choices. He was right. I've not seen straight since I met Lucy. You want Hulk? I'll get him for you. But if you hurt a hair on her head, you'll have to put me in the ground next to Hulk because I'll do anything for that woman, and that includes killing everyone who gets between us." His eyes fix on mine, and I see the promise there.

I smirk. "Get Piper back."

"You sure you wanna take Lucy?" he asks as she begins slamming her hands against the window. "She's gonna cause you a headache."

"A headache, I can handle. Missing a wife, I cannot."

I drive back towards home, leaving Michael with Tag. Lucy glares hard out the window. "Are you plotting my death?" I ask.

"I've been plotting that since you lied to me," she mutters, and I grin. "Piper probably needed some space. You really don't need to go to such drastic measures to get her attention."

"If she needed space, I'd have given her that. But she's with Hulk, the man who ripped me off."

She turns to me. "He did what?"

"He's been skimming drugs from me."

"Why would he do that? He doesn't use drugs."

I glance at her. "Because he's an idiot. Men who cross me end up dead. I gave him the benefit of the doubt because of Tag, because of you . . ." I grip the steering wheel harder. "And now, he's with my wife."

"Your wife?" she repeats.

I smirk. "She forgot to tell you that part, huh?"

"Piper agreed to marry you?" She sounds shocked.

"Hard to believe, I know, but despite what you think, I'm actually not so bad."

Lucy scoffs. "Yeah, right."

We get back to the house and Lucy stomps ahead of me. Inside, Ella is waiting in the hall. She jumps up off the steps, frowning at the sight of Lucy. "What's she doing here?" Things have been frosty between the pair since Tag chose Lucy over Ella.

"I'm collateral," Lucy mutters, shrugging.

"Does Tag know?" she asks.

"There would be no point if he didn't," I say, rolling my eyes. "What the hell were you thinking taking my wife on an adventure?"

"Piper needed to explain to Hulk. I thought it would be best if I went too, so I could keep an eye on things."

"And you thought you'd tell her tales about me and Aurora?" I growl.

She looks sheepish and shakes her head. "That was Hulk," she mumbles.

I breathe deep to keep my cool. "And how the hell does Hulk know?"

"Didn't you know that Ella and Hulk had a fling?" Lucy chimes in, and I feel my blood pressure spike. I glare at Ella, and she physically wilts before me. "Oops. Was that a secret?" asks Lucy innocently.

"You had sex with the man who's determined to ruin me?" I yell.

"It's not how it seems," mutters Ella.

"So, he forced you?" I shout, feeling the vein in my neck popping.

"No, of course not. He's not like that."

I glare at her. "Get out of my sight before I do something I'll regret." She turns to the stairs. "And show our guest to a spare room," I add. She scowls but allows Lucy to follow her.

※

I'm awoken by Ella gently shaking my arm. I sit up and pain shoots through my neck. I slept at my desk again. Checking the time, I see it's almost five in the morning. Piper's been gone for hours.

Ella thrusts her mobile phone at me. "It's Piper. She wants to talk to you."

My heart hammers in my chest as I press it to my ear. "Piper?"

"Do you love me, Anton?" she asks.

"Yes," I say firmly. I can't afford to hesitate and ruin this.

"Then please listen."

"All ears, my love."

"I need space—"

"Piper, we're married," I cut in. "We need to work this out together."

"You said you'd listen," she snaps.

I sigh, pinching the bridge of my nose. "Fine. Continue."

"I'm not saying no. I'm not walking away . . . yet. But I need some time to think things over. I know you've rationalised everything in your head, but mine's a mess."

"Are you still with him?" I ask, standing and staring out the office window.

"No," she mutters. "Tag's with me." I frown. "He told me you took Lucy."

ANTON

"Tag's orders were to bring you back here," I snap.

"Tag listened to me. He understands why I ran."

"Put him on the phone," I yell. His job isn't to understand my wife but to follow my orders.

"Let's meet and talk," she suggests, and I pause, letting her words sink in. The need to see her outweighs my anger at Tag.

"When?"

"Later today. I'll text you with a meeting place."

"Now," I tell her. "In the next hour."

"You're doing it again," she cries. "Stop pushing me."

"I have my men looking for you, Piper. I can order Tag to drag you back here kicking and screaming, but I'm being patient, agreeing to meet you and talk."

"Today at noon," she insists. "And you let Lucy go."

"I can't do that," I tell her.

"If you want to see me again, you'll do exactly that, Anton. Let her go. And stay the hell away from The Rebellion. If anything happens to them, I'm gone."

"So, now, you're threatening me?" I ask, clenching my fist by my side.

"I'm asking you."

"No harm will come to anyone if you meet me today. I'll let Lucy go once I've seen you." I disconnect the call, unwilling to barter any more. This is not how my world works. I'm not used to waiting for what I want.

Breakfast is laid out in the dining room for the first time since I sent Mum away. I guess Ella wants to get back to normal . . . well, as normal as it can be now there's just the two of us.

Ella is sitting reading the newspaper, and Lucy is opposite her picking at a croissant. They look up as I enter, and I nod in greeting, taking my seat and helping myself to a pastry. Ella pours my coffee.

"Ella said you've spoken to Piper," says Lucy.

"Yes."

"And?" she asks.

"In case you didn't realise, you're here against your will, which means I don't tell you the details of my life."

"Ella told me about the wedding," she adds, and I glare at Ella, who hangs her head. "Just

ANTON

when I think you can't get any lower, you somehow top it."

"Thank you."

"You realise Piper probably would have responded better to the old-fashioned way."

I roll my eyes. "So everyone keeps telling me."

"It's not too late to turn it around," says Ella. Lucy nods in agreement.

"She's right. Piper wants to see a better version of you."

I drop my half-eaten pastry on the plate. "I'm not sure there is a better version," I snap. "But look at you two agreeing with one another. How sweet," I say, my voice dripping with sarcasm.

"There is a better version," says Lucy, "as much as it pains me to admit it. Where's the guy who helped her when she needed it?"

"That wasn't for her. Tag asked me," I say.

"But you did it anyway. And you got her over Hulk, which was a task."

"I'm not sure that's true," I mutter, rubbing my hands over my face. "He's the first man she ran to for help."

"He was the closest at the time. But she doesn't love him," says Ella. "Not anymore."

"How can you be so sure?" I ask.

"Because he told her about him and me." She glances down at her hands and her cheeks flush. "And she wasn't upset. But when he told her about you and Aurora, she was."

"You just need to give her what she wants. Time," says Lucy gently.

Chapter Eighteen

PIPER

I wait nervously in the hotel bar. I stayed here last night, and although I had reservations about telling Anton my exact location, I figured Tag would tell him anyway.

I feel his presence before I see him. The room shifts and eyes turn towards him because he looks every bit as important as he is. His sharp suit flexes with his muscles as he moves with panther-like stealth. The gold of his Rolex catches glimmers of light, drawing attention to it, but it's the smouldering sexiness he oozes that gets the most attention from the women in the room. Even with his shades covering his dark brown eyes, he makes them swoon. He's flanked by two security guards, and as he gets closer to my table, they split off to cover the entrance and exit.

Anton stops and lifts his shades. I try not to let it affect me, even though my stomach does flips. "Let's go somewhere else and talk," he says calmly.

I smirk, shaking my head. "Sit down, Anton."

He's not amused. His left eyes twitches with the need to put me in my place, but he relents and slides into the seat opposite me. "Do you feel powerful?" he asks, glancing around the room.

"Powerful?" I repeat.

"People fear me, my love. And here you are calling all the shots, bringing me to my knees," he mutters, sounding bitter.

I smile. "I have no power, Anton. I'm just a very tired, pissed off female needing answers."

"So, ask me the questions so I can tell you the answers and we can go home."

"I'm not ready to come home, Anton," I tell him firmly.

He growls in frustration. "You're being ridiculous."

"Don't discard the way I feel," I snap.

He holds his hands up. "Sorry," he mutters.

ANTON

"The feud with The Rebellion needs to stop," I say.

He scoffs, shaking his head. "Impossible."

I push to stand, and he glares at me. "You're not even trying," I say, grabbing my bag.

He inhales deeply. "Fine, sit, we'll discuss."

I lower again. "They're my family, Anton. I can't have bad blood between us all."

"It doesn't work like that, Piper. Hulk stole from the Mafia," I hiss. "The deal we had needs to change, and Ace won't be happy with that but it's the way it has to be."

"You make the rules," I say.

"Ace knows the deal. I could've killed Hulk for what he's done," I snap, "but I let him live, and then he steals my wife."

"I made him help me."

"And he knew he was already in my debt. When my men find him . . ." He lets the sentence hang between us.

"I can't let you hurt him," I whisper.

"Because you love him?" he hisses angrily.

"No," I snap, grabbing his hand. He pulls it away. "Anton, I don't love him."

"Then stop begging for his life," he growls.

"But he's my friend," I add. "When I went to him for help last night, he was the one who talked me out of getting the next flight out of here. He told me to stay and talk to you."

"It still doesn't make up for what he's done. I have no choice."

Tears balance on my lash line. "If you hurt Hulk, you'll be hurting me. The club is my family, and I can't turn my back on them. If you kill him, you'll never be welcome there again. You'll be making me choose," I mutter.

"You're my wife, there is no choice."

"I have your money," I add, and he frowns. "The money Hulk made from selling the drugs," I add in a whisper. "He didn't spend it. I have it."

"Why are you telling me this?"

"Because you have a choice, Anton. If you continue this feud with the club, I'll take that money and I'll leave here forever. I'll keep moving so you can never find me." He clenches his jaw. "Or, you can call it off, let Hulk live, and I'll hand over the money, including my passport. I'll stay and try to work things out with you."

He stands, taking me by surprise. "I'll be in touch," he says, sliding his sunglasses back into place.

I frown. "You're leaving?"

He strides away with his bodyguards hot on his tail.

ANTON

Lucy and Ella are in the hall, sitting on the stairs, when I return. They both stand as I enter. "What?" I ask, throwing my keys on the side table and removing my shades.

"How did it go?" asks Ella.

"And can I leave yet?" Lucy adds.

"None of your business and no," I say, heading for the office.

They follow, and I groan. "You can't keep me here," snaps Lucy.

"Watch me. The deal was my wife for his, and Tag didn't bring her to me, hence why you're still here."

"You are so annoying," she hisses. "I have Abel at home."

"Did you and Piper make up?" Ella asks.

"No," I mutter coldly.

"Well, what happened?" she asks, sitting down.

"I'm not discussing it with you."

"We can help," she says, grabbing Lucy's hand and tugging her to sit.

"She makes too many demands," I snap. "Demands she doesn't understand."

"She begged for Hulk's life?" Lucy guesses, giving a smug smile when I glare at her. "What do you expect? You're messing with her family."

"He messed with me," I snarl.

"Grow up," mutters Lucy. "He stole, you know why he did it, you got the girl anyway, so what's the problem?"

"The problem is, I have to make an example, or every man and his dog will think it's okay to steal from me."

Lucy rolls her eyes. "Then kill the next man, one who isn't related to your wife."

"It's not that easy," I mutter, pouring myself a drink.

"Offer her his life for something you want," suggests Ella. "That way, you're not losing anything."

"I'm losing face," I say.

"And that's more important than Piper?" asks Lucy. "I have an idea."

"I don't want to hear it," I mutter.

"I do," says Ella.

"Offer his life for her."

"She already offered that. Sort of."

"So take it," says Lucy, shrugging. "All sorted."

"She told me she'd try," I tell her. "It's not enough."

"She needs more," says Ella. "Give her a reason to be here."

"Like?" I ask, feeling more agitated by the second.

"A job, a home." I wave my hand around, pointing out we have one of those. "It's not her home. It's our family home. Maybe suggest a job at the club?"

"Doing what exactly?"

"Management," says Lucy casually. "She's done some kind of course in that. She's great at marketing too."

I feel pissed that I didn't already know this about her. "You should both leave. I have things to discuss with the club."

"Like sparing Hulk?" asks Lucy as she stands. "Because if you hurt him, you'll blow everything."

Ace glares at me as he takes a seat at my desk. I called after I managed to talk the women into leaving me in peace. I insisted we talk, man to man, just the two of us.

"Where is he?" I ask. My men have been searching for Hulk since he and Piper ran, but he's nowhere to be found.

"Not a clue," he mutters. "He wouldn't tell me."

"She cares about him," I say bitterly. "Piper."

"She's spent a long time looking out for him. I always thought they'd end up together."

"She's asked me to let him live." Ace sits straighter, waiting for my next words. "What would you do in my shoes?" I ask, pulling out a bottle of whiskey from my desk, followed by two glasses.

"Honestly," he murmurs, "I don't know. I've been over it in my head a thousand times. He has no reason to do what he did, other than to get one over on you."

"A huge mistake on his part," I say, and Ace nods. "If I let him walk, my men will question my leadership."

"Do they know?" he asks.

"Only my closest men, but word travels."

"Then ensure it doesn't," he suggests. "If they don't know, we can deal with this between us."

"How?"

"Make him work under you."

I smirk. "You want me to employ the man who stole from me, who stole my wife?"

"Yes. He'd hate it, but maybe he'd learn something. And it would be a punishment for him, being bossed around by you all day."

I laugh, but he's right. "No offence, but I don't trust him around my wife or my sister."

"Look, he's my son, when you have your own son one day, you'll think back to this moment and realise my dilemma. If you have to take a life, take mine."

His words cause a storm in my head. "You're offering yourself over him?" I ask.

He nods. "He's in my club. I'm the leader. It should come back to me." It's noble, and something my father would never have done. "My club is my life, so are my kids. I'd do anything for them."

"I need to see him," I say. "Bring him to me tomorrow, same time. We'll come to an agreement."

***

Me: When I was ten, I watched my father beat my mother half to death.

I stare at the text before hitting send and then I knock back my drink, wincing at the throat burn. Seconds later, my phone beeps.

Piper: When I was ten, I stole my mum's tallest heels, dressed in her silk nightdress and tried to walk downstairs to show my parents how grown up I looked. I slipped, fell and broke my left ankle. Your father was an arse.

I smile before typing the next one.

Me: When I was eleven, a neighbour called the police on him. They'd heard screams from the house. She laid on the floor at his feet, cowering, and he told the police she was fine. They walked away, apologising for disturbing him. That's

ANTON

when I knew I had to grow up to be like him. The alternative was to be crushed by him knowing no one could help.

Piper: At eleven, I kissed a boy. He was smaller than me and I had to crouch down. His breath smelt like cheese and he groped my non-existent breast, telling me I was flatter than a pancake. It hurt my feelings. I hated Peter Smith. He was a prick.

Me: I know people. I'll find him. Kill him and chop off his hands.

Piper: Did your mother ever try to leave?

Me: No. Not once. She loved him. Love is blind and, in her case, that was true.

Piper: I'm sorry you had a shit father.

Hulk arrives five minutes earlier than arranged. I pour myself a drink, not bothering to offer him one. He watches as I carefully add ice and swirl it around. "Give me a reason not to kill you, Hulk."

He stands confidently. "Piper would never forgive you."

"You think I care if she forgives me?" I snap.

"Yes."

"Your father stood before me yesterday and offered himself over you," I spit. "You don't deserve him." He looks surprised by this news. "Why did you do it?"

"Because I could."

I slam my hand on the table. "Don't fucking stand here and give me nothing, Hulk, because I am so close to ending you."

"It was for her," he hisses angrily. "Because I knew you'd fuck it up and break her heart. So, I took it for her, so she could get as far away from you as she could."

I take a calming breath. "Yet you stopped her?"

"Not for you," he snaps, then he sighs. "She loves you." I sit down. "She was torn up after you forced her to tell us everything, but I see it in her eyes. She loves you, and I knew if she ran, you'd hunt her down and fuck knows how that'd end."

"I'd never hurt her," I mutter.

"You already have. I don't know how you got her down the aisle, but you did, so now she's yours. I'm stepping away."

ANTON

I scoff. "How fucking noble of you."

"Just do what you've gotta do," he snaps. "Kill me if it makes you feel better. I don't regret what I did."

"Go home, Hulk. Tell Ace he's got himself a deal."

"What's that exactly?" he asks.

I grin. "I'll let him break the news, I'm sure you'll be thrilled. You can take Lucy home too, Tag is expecting her."

Me: I was twelve when I had my first kiss. It was with Aurora when I was on holiday in Italy. We'd spend our days on the beach and our evenings with the families. We slipped away and I kissed her behind her father's house. If he'd have seen us, I would've been in trouble and we probably would've been forced to promise a marriage. She didn't let me touch her breast. Peter Smith was a lucky son of a bitch.

Piper: Maybe you were meant to be? At twelve, I had my first official boyfriend. Mainly because Peter Smith told my entire class I was easy.

Every boy in there thought they were in with a chance. His name was Andy McHale. He had floppy hair and a cute smile. He didn't kiss me for two whole weeks and when he did, it was . . . disappointing. Wet, sloppy and it gave me the ick. I dumped him the next day.

Me: Aurora and I were not meant to be. Her family has worked for mine for many years. It was a convenience. One I should have avoided.

Piper: I was thirteen when I had my first real sexual experience. His name was Dale. We'd been to a disco and he asked me to dance. He kissed me until my toes curled and said all the right things. We went on one date and he took me back to his place (his mum was out) where we checked out each other's bits with our hands. We didn't last because my dad picked me up from his place and gave him the scary warning stare. I never heard from him again.

Me: I was thirteen when I had sex. I don't remember her name. I was with my father and his men after a heavy night doing business. After those nights, we'd always go back to a club and play cards and drink. Women were never far from my father and his men. My father ordered one of them to take care of me. It was never a relationship, I don't think we even kissed.

Chapter Nineteen

♥

PIPER

Lucy and Mae insisted on meeting at the hotel, and as I wait for them to arrive, my stomach is in knots. I know they want all the details, but I'm not ready to share everything. Partly because I still feel like a fool, and partly because I don't want them to judge Anton. I don't think too much about why that is.

I stand as they arrive and wave them over to the quiet corner table I snagged us. A bottle of wine sits in an ice bucket, and I busy myself pouring it as they approach. We embrace and they sit down, taking the glasses I offer.

"So," says Mae, looking around the hotel bar, "this is nice."

ANTON

"It looks expensive," says Lucy.

"It is," I mutter.

"Then why the hell haven't you come home?" Mae demands.

"Ace told me to leave. I don't feel very welcome right now."

"And maybe you're avoiding your parents?" suggests Lucy, arching a brow.

I take a mouthful of the crisp white wine to buy me some time. I've been avoiding my mum's calls since I left the clubhouse. "I don't know what to say to them."

"Maybe start at the beginning," Mae says gently.

I take a breath. "It's all been such a whirlwind, and some of the things Anton's done haven't exactly been . . . conventional."

"Why doesn't that surprise me?" mutters Lucy.

"I just don't understand why you'd run off with a man you hardly know and marry him without telling any of us," says Mae.

Guilt hits me hard. "It wasn't planned," I whisper.

"Weddings don't just happen," Mae pushes.

"They do if you know the right people, apparently," I reply dryly. I drain my glass and refill it. "Okay," I say, "I'll tell you everything, but I don't need your judgement."

"Piper, we'd never judge you," says Mae.

"I mean of Anton too," I add. "He tricked me. I thought it was a fake wedding but turns out it wasn't."

They stare at me wide-eyed for some time before Mae finally begins to laugh. "You had me there." I stare back blankly until she stops laughing and her smile fades. "Oh my god, you're not kidding?" I shake my head.

"She's not. Ella told me," admits Lucy.

Mae glares at her. "And you didn't tell me? He can't do that," she cries. "We'll get the marriage annulled immediately."

I shake my head. "I can't. I looked into it."

"Of course, you can. You didn't know, and unless you consummate it, you can have it annulled."

I stare down at my glass. "Holy shit, you slept with him," hisses Lucy.

"I'm not proud," I admit.

"Then we'll go to the police. Someone must be able to do something," says Mae, outraged.

"He did it out of love," I explain. "I know he didn't go about it in the right way, but he meant well."

"Are you seriously defending him?" Mae snaps. "Wait until I tell Ace."

"I don't want anyone to know," I say. "This stays between us. I was just as shocked as you guys, and I've been really upset over the whole thing, but—"

"Don't you dare say you're forgiving him," snaps Lucy.

"Not exactly. I'm not ready to forgive and forget, but I'm not ready to leave him either."

Lucy groans. "The man is a pig."

"How did it go with Ella?" I ask, changing the subject.

She rolls her eyes. "It's hard to dislike her."

"I told you," I agree with a smile.

"So, do you plan to go home, either to the club or to Anton?" asks Mae.

I shrug. "I don't know. I can't stay here forever. It's costing a fortune, but it's been lovely and peaceful."

The receptionist heads our way, smiling. She stops at the table and holds out an envelope. "This just arrived for you," she tells me.

I take it, frowning. "Well, open it," Mae pushes, leaning closer.

I rip it and a set of keys falls out. I reach inside and retrieve a note. "It's an address," I say. My mobile bleeps, and I open the text.

Anton: For you. A house full of the space you require.

"Anton," I explain. "I think it's a place for me to stay."

"Well, let's go and see," says Mae excitedly.

The cab draws to a stop outside the address Anton sent me. It's an apartment block with a security entrance. We head inside, and the man behind the desk smiles. "Welcome to Eaton Apartments. How can I help?"

"Erm, I have this address," I say, passing him the note I received.

"And you have a key?" he asks. I nod, producing that too. "I'll show you up there."

We ride the elevator to the top floor, and when the doors open, I gasp. We step into a large entrance hall. "You're the only one who has access to this floor," he tells me. "Use the fob in the elevator and it'll bring you right up."

"This whole place is mine?" I ask.

He nods, smiling. "Congratulations."

He leaves, and Mae squeals excitedly. "Oh my god, he brought you a condo."

"He's buying your affection," says Lucy, shaking her head.

My phone alerts me to another text, and I smile wide when I see Anton's name.

Anton: This isn't a sex pad for your lovers. It's a place for you to rest and think about me. About us.

Me: I have no doubt you've paid the security to spy on me anyway. I'll keep all sex away from the condo.

Anton: And you'll think about us?

I tuck my phone away. He's all I think about.

The girls left hours ago and all I've done since is explore. The apartment is huge and fully furnished. There are four bedrooms, two bathrooms, and a kitchen big enough to host a party. But it feels so empty. I send a text to Anton.

Me: Are you busy?
Anton: No.
Me: Meet me for dinner?
Anton: I'll book somewhere and collect you in an hour.
Me: I know a place. No booking required. I'll send you the location and meet you there in an hour.

I'm nervous. My stomach is flopping around like its complete mush, and I feel sick. I straighten my shirt and check my reflection in the restaurant's window before entering. "Welcome to Betty's. Table for one?" a waitress asks as she roller skates towards me. I spot Anton and shake my head, passing her.

He stands as I approach. "Betty's?" he asks, raising his brows.

I laugh as he kisses me on each cheek. "You need educating on real food."

ANTON

We sit and he hands me a sticky menu, which I glance over to be polite because I already know I want a Betty special. We give our order, and the waitress skates off to get us drinks.

"You set Lucy free," I state.

He nods. "She was way more trouble than she was worth. Non-stop chatter and nagging."

I grin. "I can imagine. But Ella didn't kill her, bonus."

"No, she didn't. They actually joined forces to gang up on me." He looks me in the eye. "You look lovely."

I feel myself blush. "Thanks. You look overdressed."

He laughs, shrugging from his suit jacket and rolling up his shirt sleeves. "I didn't know Betty's was so casual."

"The apartment is . . . big."

"Space is what you asked for," he jokes. "I can always stop by if you get lonely."

I smirk. "Nice try."

"I met with Hulk today," he says, and my smile fades.

ANTON

She pales slightly at the mention of Hulk. "Don't worry, he walked away breathing." She visibly relaxes.

"What's the catch?"

"The club has had to accept different terms to our agreement. Hulk is now working for me."

"What?" she gasps.

"I like to keep my enemies close."

"You'll kill each other."

"He'll be working under me, my love. My own personal bitch."

"What does Ace think about that?" she asks.

"It was his idea. That brings me to your parents. I thought we could go and speak to them together?"

She shakes her head. "No way."

"I'm going to speak to them tomorrow anyway. If you join me, that's up to you."

"Why are you going to see them?"

"To put things right."

She pinches the bridge of her nose. "You can't just order them to accept this, Anton. They're really upset."

"You're right, I can't. But I can explain and let them decide what they accept. But either way, it won't change the outcome."

ANTON

She smiles slightly. "Wow, is this a brand new you?"

"It's the man I want to be," I mutter. "The man I'll try to be . . . for you."

Our food arrives and I eye it suspiciously. I've had burgers before, but nothing that looks like the slop served before me. I watch in amusement as Piper digs in, closing her eyes in appreciation and making the small noises I love. She catches me watching and grabs a serviette to wipe her mouth. "What?" she asks, grinning.

I shake my head. "You love food," I state. She stares down at the burger and her smile fades. I'm quick to grab her hand in mine to reassure her. "I mean it as a good thing," I tell her. "I love it. The way you appreciate every mouthful makes me smile."

She blushes slightly. "You're not impressed with the burger?" she asks, nodding at my untouched food. I take a breath before picking it up and examining it. "The trick is not to think about it too much," she says, looking amused. "Just stuff it in and enjoy."

"Enjoy?" I repeat, looking bemused.

"I promise, it's the best burger ever." She watches as I take a bite, waiting for my reaction with anticipation. I arch a brow in surprise. "Good, right?" I nod. It actually tastes pretty good. "I told you. This place might not be all fancy-shmansy like the places you go, but Betty's makes the best beef patties in the world."

We finish the food, and when the bill comes, Piper snatches it up and rushes to the counter to pay, despite my objections. "You shouldn't have paid," I tell her as we step outside.

"I asked you on the date."

"It was a date?"

"Our first official one," she confirms, hooking her arm through my own.

Michael drives us back to Piper's new place. We stop outside, and I turn to her. "I'll text you?"

"You're not coming inside?" she asks, looking disappointed.

I stroke her hair away from her face. "It's not a good idea. First date etiquette and all that."

"I thought you might want to see the place."

I smile, kissing her on the cheek. "I've seen it, mia amata. I'm meeting your parents tomorrow. If you'd like to come, let me know and I'll collect you."

ANTON

She shakes her head. "I know I'm being a coward, but I think you should see them alone first. I'm not ready to explain everything, and I'm still too hurt to answer the questions they're going to fire at me."

I nod in understanding. It's my mess, I should sort it out. "Okay. I'll call you when it's done."

The next day, Bear sits with his legs wide, his shoulders square, and his fingers pressed together in a steeple-like pose. Queenie sits by his side and twists the many gold rings that litter her fingers. She looks angry and uncomfortable. I place two drinks on the glass coffee table in front of them and take my own seat on the opposite couch. I invited them to my home rather than face the wrath of the club when everything is still very raw. It's clear I'm not welcome there right now.

"So," begins Queenie, seemingly sick of the silence, "have you brought us here to show off your nice house or to sit here in silence? Because if I was you, I'd be explaining myself right now."

Queenie doesn't scare me. In fact, she reminds me of her daughter. They have the same feistiness. I take a drink of my bourbon and smile. "I appreciate that I've done things differently to how you'd like," I begin, and Queenie's eyes bug out of her head.

"Yah think?" she huffs.

"But marrying Piper in my home country felt right."

"Home country," repeats Queenie. "Boy, you haven't lived there since you were a small child, so don't try and sell this to us like it was a sentimental dream of yours."

"I have duties," I begin.

"You took my only daughter and married her without our permission," she cuts in. "I don't give a crap about your duties or your loyalties. Nothing you say will make this right."

I shrug, relaxing back in my chair. "So, what would you like from me? I can't turn back time. Your disapproval will not change the marriage."

"You haven't even apologised," she hisses. "You don't think you've done anything wrong."

Bear finally clears his throat, and his wife looks to him. "Let me ask you this, son," he says, and his deep voice vibrates around the room. "If in the future, you have a daughter and she's just like Piper," I smile at the image, "and she runs off to another country to marry a man you don't really know that well, what will you do?"

I nod in understanding. "I'd probably kill him," I admit. "But we both know that's not going to happen."

"Don't bet on it," snaps Queenie.

I smirk. "If it's an apology you'd like, then I am sorry for whisking your daughter away to a romantic country and getting swept up in the moment."

"That's not an apology," she says. "The last time I spoke to her, she was going away with you. She didn't call to tell me about the wedding. She didn't rush to see me, full of excitement to announce how happy and in love she is. That tells me she's ashamed."

"Or she's worried about your reaction," I suggest.

"Or she realises she made a mistake," she counters.

"We're going around in circles," says Bear. "Where is Piper?"

I stare down at my drink. "She's not living here right now," I admit, and they exchange a worried look. "She asked for some space. A lot has happened recently."

"I knew it," mutters Queenie. "My little girl isn't happy."

"She's fine," I say through gritted teeth. "Things got heated with Hulk, and I let my personal feelings affect how I'd normally handle business. She was upset."

"Because she's loved that boy since she was a teenager," snaps Queenie. "Which is why we couldn't understand why the hell she suddenly married you."

"I realise that would be the preferred outcome for you," I say, irritated, "for your daughter to marry into the club. But at the end of the day, Hulk isn't the one for Piper."

"And you know that, do you?" she asks, looking amused. "Because you've seen them together?"

"He treated Piper like crap," I hiss. "He broke her heart over and over again."

"He just wasn't ready to settle down."

ANTON

Bear places his hand over Queenie's, and she presses her lips together in a firm line. "He's right, Queenie. Hulk treated her like shit."

"So, now, you're on board with this bullshit?" she snaps, turning her anger on her husband.

"I'm only interested in what Piper wants, and seeing as she's not here to tell me herself, this meeting was pointless." He rises to his feet. "When she stands in front of me, looks me in the eye, and tells me this is what she wanted, I'll shake your hand. Until then, I won't accept this marriage." He heads for the door, and Queenie gives me a smug smile before following him.

I let out a long breath and flop back in my chair. I don't know if Piper will ever be able to look her father in the eye and deliver the news he wants to hear, but I live in hope.

Chapter Twenty

♥

PIPER

Anton: I'm still alive . . . just. Your mother hates me. Your father seems undecided.

Me: I'd apologise but I feel like this is the least you deserve.

Anton: You should speak to them. Your mother misses you.

I sigh, knowing he's right, but I don't have any answers. Mum will be like a dog with a bone, and the second I stumble, she'll know something's wrong. I've thought about being honest, but they'd never forgive him, and I wouldn't blame them. I'm having trouble myself, and as sweet as the messages and the dates are, it's doing nothing to stop the hurt I feel.

Anton: Meet me today?

ANTON

Why does the thought of seeing him cheer me up?

Me: Why?
Anton: I have a proposition for you.

Anton sends Michael to collect me. We drive in silence through the busy traffic and stop outside Anton's club, the one that started this entire thing in the first place. I head inside without waiting for Michael.

It seems strange being in here when it's so empty. There's still at least seven hours until opening, and the only people around are cleaners and a few dancers practising. As I move through the bar, I spot Anton sitting in a booth, staring intently at his laptop. When I get closer, he spots me and his face lights up into a smile. He stands to greet me, kissing each cheek, then sits, indicating for me to do the same. "This feels very formal," I say.

"I want to offer you a job."

I frown. "Oh."

"I know you've always helped at the clubhouse and worked on Ace's business ventures. But I want to offer you something so you keep your independence."

"What's the catch?" I ask.

"There isn't one. I'm happy for you not to work at all, but I realise it's your decision."

"What exactly would I be doing?"

"Helping Ella out running this place," he says, looking around. "It needs fresh ideas, and I'm too busy. Ella runs the gym as well as this place. We need more help, and I like to keep it in the family."

"Are you creating this role just to keep me close?" I ask suspiciously.

He shakes his head. "No. If you turn me down, I'll advertise and hire someone. Lucy was singing your praises, and she told me you could run this place no problem." I smile. This sort of thing is my dream job, but I don't tell him that. "You'll get paid hourly like the other staff. You'll have a contract and holidays. Everything will be above-board."

"In that case, yes, I'd love to work here."

He relaxes, "Great. I'll let Ella know, and she'll arrange with you when's the best time to come

ANTON

in and talk it all over with her." He then turns his laptop towards me. He presses play and the video of my dancing begins. My smile fades. "I also wanted to make sure you saw me delete this," he adds. He clicks a button and the video disappears.

The anger I felt all those weeks ago returns. "Right," I mutter.

"I'm sorry I ever used that against you."

"I should go," I say, pushing to stand.

"Piper," he begins.

"I just..." I pause to take a breath. "I just need time."

He nods. "So you keep saying."

"What does that mean?"

"Nothing," he mutters, going back to his laptop. "I'll have Michael take you home."

"Don't bother," I say, heading for the exit.

He stands and follows. "I don't want you walking the streets with no protection."

"I'm going to the clubhouse," I tell him, and he grabs my wrist to halt me.

"Why?"

I scowl, pulling free. "To speak to Ace. To make things right with everyone."

"Including Hulk?"

"Everyone," I repeat, pulling free. "Don't you trust me?"

"I don't trust him."

I roll my eyes and continue out the door with him following. "Can I see you later?" he asks.

"I don't know. I'll see how today goes."

I get to the clubhouse, and Lucy is by the door. She screams with delight when she sees me, wrapping me in her arms. "What a nice surprise."

"I came to see Ace, straighten things out. Then I need to see my parents."

"Are you going to tell them the truth?" she asks, her eyes wide.

I shake my head. "Part truths."

Ace is behind his desk. He doesn't smile when I knock to enter but points to the chair opposite his desk. I slide into it like a naughty child. "Does Hulk know you're here?" I shake my head. "I should tell him."

"I came to see you," I say. "To ask if I can see my parents."

He frowns. "I'd never stop you seeing Bear or Queenie."

"You asked me to leave. I wasn't sure how deep that ran."

"I was angry because Hulk was upset. The best thing at the time was for you to leave. I've talked to Anton. We're straightening shit out."

"He told me Hulk will be working for him."

Ace almost smiles. "Yeah. The news didn't go down well."

"I imagine it didn't. Look, I don't know about your deals with Anton. I just came to say I'm sorry for the pain I caused. I never meant to upset anyone."

"And I'm sorry I had to ask you to leave. I never meant for that to be permanent. You're as much a part of this club as anyone. You belong here."

"I think we both know I'm outgrowing this place," I say, unable to hide the sadness in my voice. "Too much has happened between me and Hulk."

"He loves you, deep down."

"Not enough to take it further. I need more, and he can't give me that. And I don't want him to try. It's clearly not meant to be."

"So, you and Anton?"

"We're working through some stuff."

My dad bursts in and relief floods his face when he lays eyes on me. "Jesus, we've been worried sick," he growls, pulling me to stand and gripping my shoulders while he assesses me.

I laugh. "I'm fine, Pops."

Mum rushes in behind him. "Thank god."

"I texted to say I was fine," I point out.

"You know your dad likes to see you for himself."

Ace stands. "I'll let you catch up," he says, leaving the office.

We all sit. "You didn't tell us where you were staying," Mum says. "We thought you were with Anton, but then he told us you were taking a break."

I'm surprised he told them that. "I just need to get my head straight," I admit. "After Hulk and our fight, I just . . ."

"He said you aborted his baby?" she asks gently.

Shame washes over me. "It was my choice," I say firmly.

ANTON

She's quick to take my hand. "I know, I'm not judging. But why didn't you come to me? I would've supported you."

"I was scared you'd talk me into keeping it, and I wasn't ready. Neither of us were."

"You understand why we've been worried, Pip," says Pops. "You've been making strange decisions lately, acting odd."

"Things have been crazy," I say, nodding. "I'm sorry I didn't come to you and talk."

"You've always been one to bottle everything up," says Mum.

"I hate worrying you."

"So, you and Anton?" Pops asks.

"Are working through our issues."

"You shouldn't have issues when you're newlyweds," Mum snaps.

"I was drunk," I tell her, and she gasps. "I wasn't entirely clear in my thinking. And it's not Anton's fault," I say, "but I initially blamed him, thinking he was taking advantage. He didn't realise I was so drunk, so we were both at fault."

"I've warned you before about the amount you drink," Mum says.

"We can have the marriage dissolved," Pops suggests.

"I don't want to," I admit, and I smile, realising I mean it. "I want to make it work." They both look surprised. "He's not what you'd choose for me, I get it, but I love him. And he loves me, so much more than I've ever been loved."

Pops stands, pulling me to. "If you're happy, then so are we."

I nod. "I am," I reassure him.

I agree to catch-up drinks with Mae and Lucy. Three drinks in and my phone alerts me to a message.

Anton: When I was fourteen, I started down the path that would become my life. People had to fear me so I could be the man my father needed to replace him. He didn't expect it to be so soon. He thought we'd run the business together for many years.

Me: Thirteen was when I fell in love. I took a job in the club bar, only collecting glasses but it meant I could be closer to Hulk. It was the first time I felt real heartbreak. He would make a show of flirting with every club whore he could.

ANTON

It set a path of toxic behaviour we never really broke.

Anton: I never took a girlfriend. My father warned me that women would ruin me. I had to be cold, ruthless and I had to keep my head straight. Games became a thing. If Tag and I could pass it off as a dare or a bet, feelings wouldn't get involved. Everything became a game.

Me: I stopped looking beyond Hulk. The only men I ever spoke to, or kissed, were men to make him jealous. So I guess we played games too. We scored off each other's pain.

Anton: Can I see you?

Me: I don't know how long I'll be. I'm catching up with the girls.

Anton: Call me when you're done and I'll pick you up. No matter what time.

Three drinks turn to four and five, and before I know it, we're dancing on tables and blasting our favourite songs. It feels good to be back, like all my worries have gone and I'm the old me.

It's almost three in the morning when Hulk saunters in. His glazed eyes fix on me, and he scowls. "What are you doing here?"

"I came to see my parents."

He sits down, pulling me with him. "Do you know your boyfriend wants me to work for him?"

"I don't want to discuss business, Hulk. I don't know what goes on between you and him."

"He wants me to suffer. To watch you guys play happy family."

Lucy spins past us, stopping to kiss me on the cheek. "I need my bed. Goodnight." Mae's already fast asleep on the couch, so I stand.

"Me too," I say.

Hulk pulls me back to sitting. "Why would he want that when he hates me?" he asks.

"I have no idea."

He brushes the hair from my face, and I pull my head back. He scowls. "Now, I can't touch you?"

"It's not appropriate," I mutter.

"You scared you might fall under my spell?" he asks, grinning. It reminds me of what a big-headed prick he can be.

"Because I'm married," I remind him. The words feel good on my lips.

"A few days ago, you were ready to rush off to the airport. You begged me to help."

"I wasn't thinking straight," I say.

"Did you ask him about Aurora?"

I nod. "He told me the truth."

He frowns. "He admitted it?"

I nod. "And it hurt me. But we're working through it."

"Fuck, what does he give you that I don't? You wouldn't ever forgive me."

I scoff. "It happened so many times, I wouldn't know where to start the forgiveness."

He grins. "I'm a terrible boyfriend."

"Awful," I agree.

"I didn't deserve you."

"Nope." We both smile.

"For what it's worth, I'm sorry for everything."

"Me too," I whisper.

He runs his thumb over my cheek. "You're a wonderful woman. I missed out, and I'll kick myself for the rest of my life."

"You'll find the one and you'll just know she's right for you," I tell him. "I want you to be happy one day."

He presses a gentle kiss to my mouth, and I close my eyes, savouring the moment. "I love you," he whispers.

I smile, even though my eyes are filled with tears. "Goodnight."

I go to my old room and fall into the made bed. The sheets smell fresh, and I wonder if Mum cleaned them just in case I returned. I drift off into a deep sleep, feeling relaxed and happy.

ANTON

I let myself into Piper's apartment at midnight, waiting on her call that didn't come. It's almost ten a.m. when she makes an appearance.

She doesn't spot me right away, kicking the door closed and dropping her keys in the dish nearby. She kicks off her shoes and dumps her bag then heads straight to the kitchen. I hear the kettle being filled, so I make my way to her, leaning against the door frame and watching as she adds sugar to an empty cup. "Late night?" I ask, and she drops the spoon, spinning to face me with panic on her face.

"Jesus, Anton. What the hell are you doing?"

ANTON

"I was waiting for your call," I say, looking at my watch. "It never came."

She briefly closes her eyes. "Shit, I forgot. I fell asleep at the clubhouse. I'm sorry."

"Was he there?"

"At the clubhouse? Yes."

"In your bed?"

She rolls her eyes. "Not this again. I told you, there's nothing between us anymore."

"Did you talk to him?"

"Of course, I did. I spoke to lots of people, including my parents."

Rage is fuelling me, and I can't think straight. "Did he touch you?"

"In what way?" she asks, sighing.

I move closer, caging her in against the worktop. "Did any part of his body touch yours?"

"I'm not doing this, Anton," she mutters, pushing me away and storming off to the living room.

I follow. "What happened?"

"You want to know every word, every touch?" she snaps.

"Why the fuck was he touching you?" I yell.

"If you must know, he apologised for treating me so poorly. It was a nice end to a wonderful evening."

My blood boils and pounds relentlessly in my ears. "End to the evening?" I repeat.

She releases a frustrated growl. "The girls went to bed and Hulk and I had a short chat. It was five minutes. Nothing happened. He apologised, so did I, and we went our separate ways."

"Did you kiss him?" She looks away, and I ball my fists tightly. "Did you fucking kiss him?"

"Not in that way," she begins, and I'm already marching towards the door. She runs after me, slamming her body against it to block me leaving. "It wasn't like that," she yells.

"Did his lips touch yours?" I ask, my tone deadly.

"We were saying goodbye," she argues. "We were putting everything to bed."

"And to do that you had to kiss?"

"It was a short, quick goodbye kind of kiss. Not a passionate, in love kind of kiss."

"I don't know the fucking difference," I shout.

She pushes up on her tiptoes, cupping my face in her hands. She presses a light kiss to the edge of my mouth. "See, a goodbye kiss."

ANTON

Having her so close, feeling her body near mine, begins to relax me and I take a few calming breaths. She senses the change and pulls me in for another kiss, this time letting her lips linger. I part, allowing her tongue to sweep into my mouth. After a few seconds, she pulls away. "In love kiss," she confirms.

I hang my head. "I don't trust him," I mutter.

"Then trust me."

"He loves you."

"I don't love him."

"He won't stop. He wants revenge on me."

She rests her head against my chest. "The world isn't out to get you, Anton."

"I can handle the world coming for me, Piper. I can't handle it taking you."

She looks up at me. "I'm not going anywhere."

My heart stutters in my chest. "You're not?"

"I want to make it work. It means setting ground rules and boundaries, but I want us to try."

Relief floods me and I pull her against me. "That's all I want, for us to try."

"And it doesn't mean you're forgiven," she adds. "I'm still hurting over the whole wedding thing and Aurora."

"She was a mistake. I promise, it'll never happen again."

"To make us work, we have to trust each other. Don't give me a reason not to, and I won't either."

I wake with a start. Piper is on top of me, smiling down with her hair dangling over one shoulder and her naked breasts on show. She rocks against me, and I'm instantly hard. "Where will we live?" she asks.

"Here," I tell her, moving the sheets so there's nothing between us.

"What about Ella?"

"I don't want to discuss my sister right now," I mutter, watching the way her pussy rubs against my erection.

"There are enough rooms here for us all," she says.

"I'll talk to her."

"We should discuss what happens next," she suggests.

ANTON

I cup her breasts, and she closes her eyes. "I'm buying you a large diamond to make up for the lack of engagement."

"I meant our future. A wedding for my family . . . kids . . . our future."

"If you want another wedding, book it. I'll pay for whatever you want. White doves, a carriage pulled by a hundred horses . . ." I reach between us, lining myself up at her entrance. She sinks down, and I groan in pleasure.

"I'd like to wait on the kids front," she says.

I grip her waist and spin us so she's beneath me. "Not a fucking chance," I murmur, slamming into her hard. "I don't want any barriers between us. I love fucking you like this."

She laughs. "Kids are a massive barrier, Anton. I want more time with just us."

I bury my face in her neck. "When you put it like that."

Chapter Twenty-One

PIPER

I watch as Anton slips the ring box into his pocket, and I frown. "Aren't I supposed to wear that?" I ask.

"You will," he says, taking my hand and leading me from the Jewellers. Anton had arranged for the place to remain closed while I chose my ring. It was a surreal experience but one he insisted was normal. There were no prices on any on the rings, and when Anton paid, no words were exchanged.

We step out into the fresh air, and he takes my hand. It's such a normal act, yet it warms my heart. I've never had a man so openly show af-

ANTON

fection—Hulk would never have held my hand in public. Anton opens the car door, and I slide in. He joins me, again taking my hand and placing it in his lap. Michael drives us in the direction of the clubhouse, and I frown. "Aren't we going home?"

"I have to see Ace about some business," he tells me, giving my hand a gentle squeeze.

When we step into the clubhouse ten minutes later, there's hardly anyone around, which is unusual for this time of day. Anton checks his phone. "Ace is out back. I won't be long," he tells me, kissing me gently on the cheek and rushing off.

I take a seat on the couch. The place feels eerie without the guys yelling or the kids running around. After ten minutes, I sigh loudly and get to my feet, heading out to find Anton. I shove the back door and gasp. Everyone is right there, staring back at me, and right in front of the crowd is Anton.

"About time," he says, grinning as he drops down onto one knee. I stare wide-eyed. "Piper, love of my life, my one and only, will you marry me?" He produces the ring.

I bite my lower lip, fighting the smile trying to break through. "Aren't we already past that?"

"Give the man an answer," says Ace, laughing.

I nod. "Yes, of course, I'll marry you . . . again."

He stands, placing the ring on my finger and pulling me closer. "Is now a good time?"

I frown. "I don't understand."

The crowd separates to reveal rows of chairs already set up, dressed in white ribbons and running either side of a red carpet. At the front, there's a vicar, and he gives a small smile. "Will you remarry me right now?" asks Anton.

"But I . . . this is so . . ."

Mae grabs my hand. "Sudden, we know, but when has Anton ever worried about that? Come, we have your dress upstairs."

"Upstairs?" I repeat as she drags me back inside the clubhouse followed by the other women.

"We have half an hour to turn you into a bride," says Mum.

We get upstairs to my mum's room, where there's a dress bag hanging up. "Who chose this?" I ask warily, hoping to God it wasn't my mum. Her wedding dress was like a frilly toilet roll holder.

ANTON

"Anton," says Lucy, arching a brow. "We weren't allowed to peek."

I take a deep breath as Mum guides me to stand in front of the dress. She then proceeds to unzip the bag. When it falls away, I stare wide-eyed, and the women around me gasp. It's stunning. I run my finger over the boned white bodice covered in tiny glistening diamante's. "We don't have time to stare," says Mae, pushing me into a chair. "Makeup and hair," she orders.

I take a deep breath and hook my arm into Pops'. "Are you sure about this, baby girl?" he asks. "I can bust you out of here and have you on a plane before he notices you're gone."

I laugh. "Did he ask your permission this time?"

He nods. "He came to see me last night."

"And you gave your blessing?"

He shrugs. "Like I said, it ain't too late to get you out of here."

I stand on my tiptoes, and he lowers to meet my kiss on his cheek. "I love you, Pops. Thank you for giving your blessing."

"As long as you're happy," he says, staring into my eyes.

I nod. "Very happy."

"Then let's do this."

ANTON

How the fuck I pulled this off in twenty-four hours is beyond me, but here we are, and as I take in the many faces around me, I know I've done the right thing. Piper needed this and so did her family. Even Hulk made the effort to turn up, not that he looks happy about it.

The door opens and Bear steps out. I hold my breath for a second until she appears behind him. Tag slaps me hard on the back. "Shit, she looks hot," he whispers.

I grin. "Careful, that's my wife you're talking about."

She makes her way towards me. Her smile is infectious, and I stop myself from marching to her and making her walk faster. She stops before me and her father kisses her on the cheek before turning to me and holding out his hand.

ANTON

I stare for a second before taking it firmly and shaking it. "Take care of her," he warns me.

I nod. "Of course."

I take Piper by the hand, and we turn to the vicar. I paid over the odds to get him here to do this blessing, and as he reads out his words, I stare at Piper's side profile, unable to take my eyes off her. She's worth every penny and more.

The service is brief. We exchange rings—I chose silver bands when we returned from Italy—and when I slide Piper's in place, I feel truly relaxed. She's officially my wife. And in true Rebellion style, the service is followed by a celebration which Bear and Queenie insisted on despite me wanting to get Piper home so I could have her to myself.

Darkness fell over two hours ago, but that isn't enough to stop a biker celebration. I watch my wife dancing with her friends and take a drink of my whiskey. "How does it feel?" asks Tag, joining me.

"Amazing."

"If someone told me ten years ago this is where we'd be now, I'd have laughed," he says.

"It feels like we were always meant to be here."

I pull out my mobile.

Me: At thirty, I married the most amazing woman. She ruined me for any other woman from the minute I met her. I spent weeks trying to get her attention, but she was too busy loving a guy who didn't love her back. So I did a terrible thing...

I see her take her phone out of her bra and I laugh to myself. She reads the text, smiling and glancing my way.

Piper: At twenty-five, I married a man who came into my life like a force. He's the perfect man for me, yet I never saw it until recently. What was the terrible thing?

Me: I forced her to notice me. I didn't care who I hurt in the process because I was desperate to have her to myself.

Piper: It must have worked if you married her...

Me: I'm a very lucky man. She forgave me even though I didn't deserve it. And now she's mine, I'm the luckiest man alive.

ANTON

Piper: We should probably stop texting. I don't think my husband would like it. Especially now I'm with child...

I stare at the message for a solid minute, allowing her words to soak in. When I look up, she's standing before me. "Congratulations," she whispers, smiling.

I stand, taking her face in my hands. "You're having my baby?" She nods, and my heart hammers in my chest. "Are you okay with that?" I ask.

"Yes," she murmurs, pressing a kiss to my lips. "When I did the test, I was praying for a positive. It surprised me," she admits. "I'm ready, I just didn't know it."

I sweep her against me, swinging her around. She laughs, clinging to me. "I love you so much," I whisper, kissing her gently.

"I love you too, marito," she says, and I laugh.

"You're practising Italian?"

She shrugs, grinning. "It sounds sexy."

"Un linguaggio sexy per una donna sexy," I say against her lips. "A sexy language for a sexy lady."

NICOLA JANE

The End

About the Author

I'm a UK author, based in Nottinghamshire. I live with my husband of many years, our two teenage boys and our four little dogs. I write MC and Mafia romance with plenty of drama and chaos. I also love to read similar books. Before I became a full-time author, I was a teaching assistant working in a primary school.

If you'd like to follow my writing journey, join my readers group on Facebook, which you'll find on the next page.

Social Media

♥

You can visit my website where you'll find information about my latest projects, signed paperbacks and regular updates.

https://www.authornicolajane.com/

I love to hear from my readers and if you'd like to get in touch, you can find me here . . .

My Facebook Page
My Facebook Readers Group
Bookbub
Instagram
Goodreads
Amazon

Also by Nicola Jane

♥

The Kings Reapers MC
Riggs' Ruin https://mybook.to/RiggsRuin
Capturing Cree https://mybook.to/CapturingCree
Wrapped in Chains https://mybook.to/WrappedinChains
Saving Blu https://mybook.to/SavingBlu
Riggs' Saviour https://mybook.to/RiggsSaviour
Taming Blade https://mybook.to/TamingBlade
Misleading Lake https://mybook.to/MisleadingLake

Surviving Storm https://mybook.to/Surviving Storm
Ravens Place https://mybook.to/RavensPlace
Playing Vinn https://mybook.to/PlayingVinn

<u>The Perished Riders MC</u>
Maverick https://mybook.to/Maverick-Perished
Scar https://mybook.to/Scar-Perished
Grim https://mybook.to/Grim-Perished
Ghost https://mybook.to/GhostBk4
Dice https://mybook.to/DiceBk5
Arthur https://mybook.to/ArthurNJ

<u>The Hammers MC (Splintered Hearts Series)</u>
Cooper https://mybook.to/CooperSHS
Kain https://mybook.to/Kain
Tanner https://mybook.to/TannerSH

Printed in Dunstable, United Kingdom